"Your fat
place you ll be sale is Texas...

"Then you should listen to my father," Dixie said, eyes blazing with anger before she spun around and headed out the deck door, slamming it behind her.

Chance swore as he watched her walk to the edge of the railing, her back to him. The light breeze stirred her hair. He could see her breath coming out in small white puffs. Forty-eight hours. Hadn't Bonner told him not to let Dixie get to him? Just find her and take her to the plane. Period. Bonner had said it was a family matter. Let them work it out. It had nothing to do with him. Hell, what were the chances that anyone was really trying to kill her anyway...?

KEEPING CHRISTMAS

B.J. DANIELS

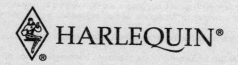

HARLEQUIN®

TORONTO • NEW YORK • LONDON
AMSTERDAM • PARIS • SYDNEY • HAMBURG
STOCKHOLM • ATHENS • TOKYO • MILAN • MADRID
PRAGUE • WARSAW • BUDAPEST • AUCKLAND

This one is for my Uncle Jack Johnson,
whom we lost this year. Jack will be greatly missed,
especially his big heart, his laugh and his Texas barbecue.

ISBN-13: 978-0-373-22953-6
ISBN-10:   0-373-22953-4

KEEPING CHRISTMAS

Copyright © 2006 by Barbara Heinlein

ABOUT THE AUTHOR

A former award-winning journalist, B.J. Daniels had thirty-six short stories published before her first romantic suspense, *Odd Man Out*, came out in 1995. Her book *Premeditated Marriage* won the *Romantic Times BOOKclub* Best Intrigue award for 2002, and in the same year she received the magazine's Career Achievement Award for Romantic Suspense. B.J. lives in Montana with her husband, Parker, two springer spaniels—Scout and Spot—and a temperamental tomcat named Jeff. She is a member of Kiss of Death, the Bozeman Writers' Group and Romance Writers of America. When she isn't writing, she snowboards in the winters and camps, water-skis and plays tennis in the summers. To contact her, write P.O. Box 183, Bozeman, MT 59771 or look for her online at www.bjdaniels.com.

Books by B.J. Daniels

CAST OF CHARACTERS

Chance Walker—Tracking down Southern spitfire Dixie Bonner before Christmas should have been easy for the private investigator.

Dixie Bonner—When she found some old snapshots hidden in her mother's jewelry box, Dixie had no idea of the danger—or that the trail would lead her to Montana to the man she'd always loved.

Beauregard Bonner—He'd kept the truth from his daughters all these years. But now not only was the secret out, it had unleashed a killer and an even bigger secret.

Rebecca Lancaster Bonner—All she ever wanted was to shed her family's white-trash past and be one of Houston's high society. How far would she go, though, to make sure no one ever found out the truth about her?

Oliver Lancaster—There were only two things in the world that got his blue blood going: money and power. Unfortunately, he stood to lose both unless his luck changed.

Carl Bonner—He'd always lived in his younger brother's shadow. Everyone thought Carl had reason to resent Beauregard. Others thought he was just biding his time until he could get even.

Ace Bonner—It was hell being the poor, looked-down-upon cousin of Beauregard Bonner.

Prologue

The rain had stopped, but the parking garage seemed unusually cold and dark as Dixie Bonner started to step from the elevator.

One booted foot poised on the edge of the concrete, she hesitated, sensing something was wrong. She stood listening for whatever sound had alerted her, only now aware of how late it was. The library had closed for the night as had all the other businesses around it except the coffee shop back up the street where she'd been the past few hours.

She hadn't realized the time or noticed how dark and empty the streets were. All the holiday shoppers had gone home for the night. She'd foolishly paid no attention because she'd had other things on her mind.

Now she felt vulnerable. Not that she wasn't used to taking chances. It went with her job. But taking chances was one thing. Just being plain dumb was another.

She let one hand drop to her shoulder bag as she eased back, but kept her free hand holding the elevator doors open as she scanned the parking garage.

Her fingers found the purse's zipper and began to slowly glide it open, speeding up as she heard the scrape of a shoe sole on the concrete floor of the garage.

She was in danger, but then she'd suspected that the moment the elevator doors had opened. She'd been on edge all night, at one point almost certain someone had been watching her beyond the rain-streaked window of the coffee shop.

There were two vehicles left in the unattended garage. A tan cargo van and her fire-engine-red Mustang. The van was parked right next to the Mustang.

Her hand closed over the can of pepper spray in her purse as she debated making a run for her car or returning to the upper level of the parking garage. Neither seemed prudent.

The decision was made for her as a man wearing a black stocking mask suddenly appeared in the open elevator doorway. A gun glinted in his right hand. She hit the door close button at the same time she brought up the can of pepper spray and pointed it at the man's face.

He let out a howl and stumbled back as the full force of the pepper spray hit him in the eyes and soaked into the mask.

She shoved past him through the closing elevator doors, her eyes tearing from being in close counters with the spray. Running, near blind, tears streaming down her face, she sprinted toward the red blur of her car.

Too late she sensed movement out of the corner of her eye. A second masked man tackled her and took her down hard, knocking the air from her lungs. She landed on her stomach, gasping for breath even before he jammed his knee into her back to hold her down.

She still had the pepper spray can in one hand, a tight grip on her purse in the other. But she had a bad feeling that these men weren't after her purse.

She tried to yell for help, knowing it was senseless. There was no one around. No one would hear her cries even if she had enough breath to scream.

Strong fingers twisted the pepper spray from her hand. She heard the can land where the man threw it, the can rolling away into the silence of the vacuous parking garage.

With her face pushed into the gritty cold-damp concrete, she could see nothing but the tires of her car next to her. She'd almost made it to safety.

She heard the first man come running up.

"Bitch." He cursed. "My face is friggin' on fire."

She heard the anger in his voice and knew things were about to get a whole lot worse. The kick caught her in the ribs. The pain was excruciating, her cry pitiful, as the air was knocked out of her again.

She gasped for breath, fighting the terror that now had a death grip on her. She didn't stand a chance against two men. Not alone in this garage. With a sabbatical from work and her lousy relationship with her family, it could be weeks before anyone even realized she was missing.

"Stop!" the second man ordered. "For hell's sake don't kill her yet. We have to find out where she put the damned journal and the disks before you—"

The second blow was to her head. Pain glittered behind her eyes just before the darkness.

DIXIE WOKE IN blackness, her head throbbing, her body cramped. She shifted position, bumped an elbow and a knee, and started to panic, gasping for breath as she realized she was in a cramped dark space.

She fought not to panic, not to let her mind tell her that her small prison was slowly closing in on her.

Breathe. You're alive. Temporarily. *Breathe.*

"Just bring the damned computer and all the disks you can find." It was the voice of the second man from the parking garage.

"I thought it was supposed to look like a robbery," the first demanded.

"You let me take care of that. What about her journal? Have you found it yet?"

"It's not in here."

She heard the sound of footfalls heavy nearby as if someone was treading up stairs. She held her breath, trying to calm her breathing, her panic.

Her fingers moved slowly, cautiously, along the inside of the space around her. She frowned, feeling cool metal, rough carpet. She could hear the sound of things breaking, larger things being knocked over. She sniffed and caught a familiar scent. Laundry detergent. She'd bought a box at the market earlier and put it—

She was in the trunk of her car!

The realization sent a shot of hope racing through her. Hurriedly, she oriented herself, scrunching her body to get her feet against the rear seat, the one with the broken latch. She could hear voices. The two men arguing.

Bracing her body against the opposite side of the

trunk, her feet against the rear seat, she pushed with all her strength.

At the sound of a loud crash, she kicked the seat hard. The latch gave, the seat flopped down.

Through the hole came light. She wiggled around until she could peer out. The car was parked in her garage. The two men were inside her house, the adjoining door open.

She listened, afraid they would come back now. No sound. Had they heard her?

She moved fast, half afraid they would be standing outside her car amused at the futility of what she thought was her great escape. But she had *no* chance cramped in the trunk. She didn't have much chance in the back seat. But even a little edge was better than nothing.

Slithering through the space with the seat down, she ducked behind the front seats and looked out. No sign of the men in the garage. The door to the house was still open, but she couldn't see anything but light coming from the kitchen. Where were the men?

She heard the sounds of more objects breaking, things being knocked over and destroyed. She grabbed the back door handle and, as quietly as possible, popped it open.

Inside the house she heard another crash, then voices. She slipped out of the car, making the decision just as quickly. The keys were in the ignition. She opened the driver's side door, slid behind the wheel and locked all four doors as she reached for the garage door opener and said a silent prayer.

The garage door began to lift slowly and noisily as she fired up the car's engine, her eyes on the door leading into the house.

The overhead garage door was too slow. Hurry! She had the car in Reverse, engine revved, ready, her gaze flicking nervously from the slowly rising garage door to the open door to the house. The garage door was a third of the way up. Just a little higher.

The two men came flying out of the house, stumbling down the steps that dropped into the garage. One of them slammed into the side of her car and groped for the door handle.

The garage door was almost up enough. The second man shoved past him, a gun in his hand. The man with the gun started to raise the weapon as she tromped down on the gas. The car shot backward under the rising garage door, the antenna snapping off.

She thought she heard a shot as she swung the car around in the driveway, slammed it into first and took off, tearing across the lawn, jumping the curb, tires squealing as they met pavement, engine screaming.

She hadn't realized she'd been holding her breath until it came out on a sob. She was shaking so hard, she could hardly hold on to the steering wheel. But she kept going. They would be coming after her. She'd seen the van parked just down the street from her house.

Worse, she'd seen their faces.

She'd known in the parking garage that they'd planned to kill her. But now they had no choice.

She'd recognized one of them—and he knew it.

Chapter One

All Chance Walker wanted was to get to the cabin before the snowstorm and the holiday traffic got any worse.

He'd only stopped in for a minute, but now he couldn't wait to get home. He glanced around his office, ignoring the dust that had accumulated while he'd been gone. The light was flashing on his antiquated answering machine. For a moment he thought about checking his calls.

But it was only days until Christmas and he told himself he wasn't in the mood for anything to do with work. Anyone he wanted to talk to knew he hadn't been in his office for weeks and wouldn't be for a while longer. The only reason he'd stopped by this evening was to gather up any bills from the floor where the mailman had dropped them through the old-fashioned door slot.

Chance nudged his dog awake with the toe of his boot. From in front of the old radiator, Beauregard lifted his head and blinked at him, the dog not looking any more anxious to go out in the cold than Chance was.

"Come on, boy. Once we get to the cabin I'll build us a fire and make us both big fat steaks. It's the holidays. I think we deserve a treat."

The dog keyed on the word "treat" and jumped to his feet, padding to the door, tail wagging.

Chance glanced around the office one last time to make sure he hadn't missed anything, not sure when he'd be back. The private investigator business was slow this time of year in Montana and he knew he hadn't completely recuperated from the bullet Doc had taken out of his shoulder.

While the physical wound had healed, Chance's heart wasn't into work yet. He wasn't sure when he would be again. Certainly not until the holidays were long gone. This time of year was always the toughest for him.

He saw Beauregard's ears perk up as they both heard the outside door open. Chance didn't give it a thought since he shared the building with a beauty salon, an insurance firm, investment office and a knitting shop.

With Christmas just days away, he knew the beauty shop and knitting store had been busy. That would explain the small, slowly melting snowdrift that had formed just inside his door. With the main entrance door opening and closing all the time, gusts of snow blew up the hallway and under his office door. He'd turned down the heat in his absence, planning to hide out until after the holidays and things slowed down again in his building.

He picked up his old black Stetson from his desk and snugged it down on his head, then moved to open the door, turning out his office lights as he and Beauregard stepped into the long hallway.

At the other end, a bundled-up figure had just come in. Snowflakes, light as feathers, skittered along the wood floor as the man shut the front door behind him, closing out the snowy December evening and the sound of a bell jingler nearby.

Chance slammed his office door, checking to make sure it was locked, and started down the hallway.

The man hadn't moved. Probably waiting for his wife in the beauty salon or the knitting shop.

But as Chance drew closer, he felt a familiar prickle of unease. The man was good-size, huddled in a sheepskin coat, fine boots and slacks, his face in shadow under a pale gray Stetson. A wealthy Montana rancher or— Chance felt a start and swore under his breath.

Or a rich Texas oilman.

"Chance Walker," the man drawled in a familiar, gravely voice.

Next to Chance the dog let out a low growl as the hair stood up on the back of the canine's neck.

"Easy, Beauregard," Chance said as he reached down to pet the mutt, surprised his dog had the same reaction Chance did to the man.

"You named your dog Beauregard?"

"Couldn't think of a better name for a stray, mean-spirited mongrel."

Beauregard Bonner let out of howl of laughter and thrust out his hand, grabbing Chance's and pulling him into a quick back-slapping hug. "Damn, boy, I've missed you." Beauregard, the dog, growled louder in warning. "Call off your dog and tell me where we can get a stiff drink in this town. You and I need to talk."

Chance couldn't imagine what he and Beauregard Bonner might have to talk about. The last time Chance had seen Bonner it had been in the man's Texas mansion outside of Houston. Bonner had been gripping a shotgun and threatening to blast a hole the size of Texas in him.

"Damn, this is a cold country," Bonner said, rubbing his gloved hands together and grinning good-naturedly, but there was a nervous edge to the man that Chance didn't miss. "I don't know about you, but I really could use that drink."

Chance had a feeling he would need one himself. He pointed to the Stockman Bar across the street, his curiosity getting the better of him. What would bring a man like Bonner all the way to Montana in the middle of winter?

Nothing good, of that Chance was certain as they crossed the street in the near blizzard, the dog trotting along beside them.

"They let dogs in bars up here?" Bonner asked in surprise as the dog followed them through the door and down the long bar to sprawl on the floor under Chance's stool.

"Actually, they prefer dogs over Texans," Chance said.

Bonner looked over at him with a Don't Mess With Texas scowl. "I don't care how long you've lived here, you're still a Texan, born and raised."

Chance said nothing as Bonner ordered them both a drink. Bonner still drank expensive Scotch neat. Chance had a beer, nursing it since he had the drive ahead of him to the cabin—and he knew to keep his wits about him as he studied the man sitting on the stool next to him with growing dread.

Beauregard Bonner had aged since Chance had last seen him. His blond hair had grayed and the lines around his eyes had deepened. But the booming drawl was that of the filthy rich oilman Chance remembered only too well.

"Guess you're wondering what I'm doing here," Bonner said after downing half of his drink.

Chance stared down into his beer, waiting. A Christmas song was playing on the jukebox and the back bar glittered with multicolored lights. There was a Christmas tree decorated with beer cans at the other end of the bar and a large Santa doll with a beer bottle tucked in his sack.

"It's my daughter," Bonner said.

Chance's head shot up. "Rebecca?" Last he'd heard, Rebecca had married some hotshot lawyer from back east who'd gone to work for her father. They lived in a big house near Houston and had three kids.

"Not Rebecca." Bonner made a face. "*Dixie.*"

"Dixie?" Rebecca's little sister? Chance recalled freckles, lots of them, braces and pigtails, an impish little kid who'd been a real pain in the neck the whole time he'd been dating Rebecca.

"Dixie might be in some trouble," Bonner said as he scowled down at his drink.

Chance could not for the life of him imagine what that had to do with him and said as much.

"I want to hire you to find her."

Chance pulled back, even more surprised. "They don't have private investigators in Texas?"

"She's not in Texas. She's in Montana. At least, it's where the last kidnapper's call came from."

Chance swore. *"Kidnapper?"*

"I need you to find her. I'm worried this time because the ransom demand is a million dollars."

"This time? What was it *last* time?" Chance asked, half joking.

"When Dixie was three, it was a hundred dollars. Then a hundred thousand in high school. Five hundred grand in college. I figured Dixie was too smart to ever ask for a million, but damned if she didn't."

Chance couldn't believe this. "Have you contacted the police? The FBI? Shouldn't someone be looking for her?"

"There's something you have to understand about Dixie. The last time she had herself kidnapped in college, I had cut off her money over a little dispute between us. The FBI got involved. It was ugly. She was dating some loser…" He drained his drink and signaled the bartender for another.

Chance motioned that he was fine. "Loser?" he repeated, remembering when Bonner had called him the same thing. It was about the time he'd started dating Dixie's older sister Rebecca. Chance supposed Bonner would still consider him just that, a loser. So why come all this way to hire *him?*

Rubbing a hand over his face, Chance asked, "So you're saying that Dixie hasn't really been kidnapped. You're sure about that?"

"I can't be sure of anything with Dixie." Bonner tipped up his glass and swallowed. "That's why I want you to find her. I trust you more than I do the police or the FBI, and you can do it with more discretion."

Chance shook his head. "For starters, I don't have the resources of either of those agencies and I'm not working right now. I'm taking the holidays off."

Bonner nodded. "Heard about you getting shot." He smiled at Chance's reaction. "I've kept my eye on you over the years."

Nothing could have surprised Chance more, but he did his best to hide it. "Then you know that I'm not taking any cases right now."

"I know you almost got killed, but that the guy who shot you is dead and won't be hurting anyone else thanks to you," Bonner said.

"Don't try to make killing a man a virtue, all right?"

"You had no other choice," Bonner said. "I saw the police report. Also, I know that your shoulder is as good as new." He smiled again, a twinkle in his eye. "Money talks…"

Chance swore under his breath. Bonner hadn't changed a bit. He believed he could buy anything—and most of the time he could. Bonner's was a famous Texas story. Raised on a chicken-scratch farm, poor as a church mouse, Beauregard Bonner had become filthy rich overnight when oil had been discovered on the place his old man had left him.

Ever since, Bonner had used his money to control as many people as possible. And vice versa if what he was saying about his youngest daughter was true.

"Go to the authorities," Chance said irritably. "You've come to the wrong man for this one."

"I can't," Bonner said, looking down into his drink again. "They wouldn't take it seriously. Why should they, given that she's pulled this stunt before and there is no evidence that she's been abducted?"

"What about the ransom demand and the fact that she's missing? There was a ransom demand, right?"

"Just a male voice over the phone demanding a million dollars before I even knew she *was* missing," Bonner said. "I thought it was a joke. The call came from a pay phone in Billings, Montana."

Chance studied the older man for a long moment. "What is it you aren't telling me?"

Bonner sighed. "Just that I need her found as quietly as possible. I'm involved in some deals right now that are sensitive, which I'm sure is why she's doing this now."

Chance stared at the man. "You're telling me your business deal is more important than your daughter?"

"Don't be an ass, of course not," Bonner snapped. "Don't you think I pulled a few strings to find out what I could? All the recent charges on Dixie's credit cards have what they say is her signature. From the pattern of use it would appear that she's up to her old tricks."

Chance groaned. "She's *kidnapped* herself?" Again. Why did she have to pick Montana this time, though? "Why don't you just give her the million? Hell, she's going to inherit a lot more than that someday anyway, right?"

Bonner looked over at him and shook his head. "She'd just give it all away. To save some small country somewhere. Or a bunch of damned whales. Or maybe free some political prisoners. She's like my brother Carl. I swear it's almost as if they feel guilty that we have money and want to give it all away."

"Generosity, yeah, that's a real bad trait. No wonder you're so worried."

Bonner ignored the jab. "You don't know Dixie."

No, he didn't. Or at least he hadn't since she was twelve. Nor was he planning to get to know the grown-up version.

He pushed away his beer and stood, Beauregard the dog getting quickly to his feet—no doubt remembering the promise of a treat once they got to the cabin. "Sorry, but you'll have to get someone else. When you came in, I was just closing up my office for the rest of the holidays and going to my cabin."

"The one on the lake," Bonner said without looking at him.

Chance tried to tamp down his annoyance. Clearly Bonner had been doing more than just keeping track of him all these years. Just how much had he dug up on him? Chance hated to think.

"I know about the cabin you built there," Bonner said, his gaze on his drink, his voice calm, but a muscle flexed in his jaw belying his composure. "I also know you need money." He turned then to look at Chance. "For your medical bills. And your daughter's."

Chance felt all the air rush out of him. He picked up the beer he'd pushed away and took a drink to give himself time to get his temper under control.

It didn't work. "You wouldn't really consider using

my daughter to get me to do what you want, would you?" he asked through gritted teeth.

Bonner met his gaze, but something softened in his expression. "Dixie is a hellion and probably payback for what a bastard I've been all of my life, but she's my *daughter*, Chance. My flesh and blood, and I'm scared that this time she really *is* in trouble."

Chapter Two

Chance drove to his cabin, Beauregard sitting next to him on the pickup's bench seat, panting and drooling as he stared expectantly out at the blizzard.

On the seat between him and the dog was the manila envelope Beauregard Bonner had forced on him. Chance hadn't opened it, had barely touched it—still didn't want to.

Snow whirled through the air, blinding and hypnotic, the flakes growing larger and thicker as the storm settled in. He drove the road along the edge of the lake, getting only glimpses of the row of summer cabins boarded up for the season until he came to the narrow private road that led to his cabin.

His cabin was at the end of the road. He shifted into four-wheel drive, bucking the snow that had already filled the narrow road. Although mostly sheltered in pines, his cabin had one hell of a view of the lake. That's why he'd picked the lot. For the view. And the isolation. There were no other cabins nearby. Just him and the lake and the pines stuck back into the mountainside.

He was still mentally kicking himself as he pulled up behind the cabin and cut the engine. He wasn't sure who he was angrier at, himself or Beauregard Bonner. He couldn't believe he'd taken the job. The last person on earth he wanted to work for was Bonner—not for *any* amount of money.

But Bonner, true to form, had found Chance's weakness. And Chance had been forced to swallow his pride and his anger, and think only of how the outrageous amount of money Bonner was offering him would help take care of the medical bills.

Not that the whole thing hadn't put him in a foul mood. And it being so close to Christmas, too.

He sat in the pickup, listening to the ticking of the engine as it cooled, taking a moment to just stare out at his cabin, the storm and what little he could see of the frozen white expanse of lake that stretched for miles.

Nothing settled him like this place. He'd built the cabin with his own hands, every log, every stone. His daughter had been born here on a night much like this one.

Beauregard pawed at his arm, no doubt wondering what the hold up was on that treat. "Sorry, boy." Chance smiled as he reached over and rubbed the dog's big furry head. Beauregard really was the ugliest dog Chance had ever seen. A big gangly thing, the dog was covered with a mottled mass of fur in every shade of brown. But those big brown eyes broke your heart. Two pleading big brown eyes that were now focused on him.

Chance had found him beside the road, starving and half dead. He'd seen himself in the dog—the mutt was the most pathetic thing Chance had ever laid eyes on.

He'd worn no collar, had apparently been on his own for a long time, and hadn't had the best disposition. Clearly they were two of a kind and meant to be together.

"I know," Chance said, opening his pickup door. "I promised a treat." The moment he'd said the word treat, Chance knew it had been a mistake.

Beauregard bounded over the top of him, knocking the beat-up black Stetson off Chance's head as the dog bolted out the door and along the walkway to the deck at the front of the cabin.

Laughing, Chance got out, as well, retrieving his Stetson and slapping the snow from it as he followed the dog. On his way, he grabbed an armful of firewood and took a moment to pause as he always did to say a prayer for his daughter.

REBECCA BONNER LANCASTER pressed her slim body against the wall in the dark hallway, feeling nothing like the Southern belle she pretended to be.

She could hear her husband on the phone, but was having trouble making out what he was saying.

It was hard for her to believe that she had stooped this low. Spying on her husband. What would her friends at the country club think? Most of the time, she couldn't have cared less what Oliver was up to.

Everyone in Houston knew he'd had his share of affairs since they'd been married. She suspected that most wives pretended not to know because it came as relief. As long as he left her alone, it was just fine with her.

As the daughter of Beauregard Bonner, she had her friends, her charity work, her whirlwind schedule of social obligations. That kept her plenty busy. Not to mention overseeing the nanny, the housekeepers and the household.

Rebecca couldn't say she was happy, but she was content. She doubted most women could even say that. No, she told herself, no matter what her husband was up to, she'd made the right decision marrying Oliver Lancaster.

Oliver came from a family with a good name but no money, and while the Bonner's had money, they didn't have the pedigree. Because of that, it had been a perfect match. Oliver had opened doors that had been closed to her and her family. He was good-looking, charming and tolerant of her family and her own indiscretions.

Of course, her money helped. That, and his prestigious job working for her father. She knew Oliver didn't really "do" anything as legal consultant at Bonner Unlimited. The truth was he'd barely passed the bar and provided little consulting to her father. Beauregard had a team of high-paid lawyers, the best money could buy, when he really needed a lawyer.

But Oliver didn't seem to mind being paid to do nothing. And the title didn't hurt in social circles either.

"What?" she heard her husband demand to someone on the phone.

Rebecca held her breath. For days now she'd noticed something was bothering Oliver. She'd hinted, asked, even had sex with him, but whatever it was, he was keeping it to himself.

So, she'd gone from snooping through his suit pockets to eavesdropping on his phone conversations.

Oliver swore. She could hear him pacing, something he only did when he was upset with her or her father.

"What the hell did he do that for?" Oliver demanded into the phone, then lowered his voice to ask, "Where is he now?"

Rebecca frowned, wondering who Oliver was talking about.

"That son of a bitch," Oliver swore again.

There was only one person Oliver referred to in that tone and in those exact words. Her father. What had Daddy done now? She closed her eyes, relieved there was nothing more to it than Oliver finding fault with her father.

"Montana?" Oliver said.

Rebecca's eyes flew open.

"What the hell is he doing in Montana?"

Daddy was in Montana?

"You've got to be kidding me. That damned Dixie."

Dixie?

Her husband had moved to the other end of the room now, his voice muffled. She slipped along the wall silent as a cat, knowing it would be ugly if she got caught. And Oliver hated ugly scenes.

She could hear him talking, but still couldn't make out most of the words. Then she heard a name that stopped her cold.

Chance Walker.

Daddy was in Montana and it had something to do with her sister Dixie and Chance Walker?

All the breath rushed out of her. She hadn't heard Chance's name in years. She'd completely forgotten about him. Well, maybe not completely. But she had been sure her father had.

What possible reason would Daddy and Dixie have for going to Montana—let alone that it involved Chance Walker?

"Don't worry, I will. As long as nothing holds up the deal. I told you, you can count on me. No, no, I believe you. As long as you say it isn't going to be a problem. All right. If you're sure."

Rebecca was shaking so hard she could barely catch a breath. Chance Walker. She'd thought she'd never hear that name again. But now that she had, she felt sick as it brought back the memory of the choice she'd made so many years ago—and why.

As Oliver hung up the phone, Rebecca retreated down the hall as quickly and quietly as possible. He was the last person she wanted to see right now.

AFTER CHANCE HAD a big roaring fire going in the stone fireplace, he spotted the manila envelope where he'd tossed it on the table. It wasn't too late to call Bonner to tell him he'd changed his mind.

Every instinct told him that Bonner was holding out on him. He hadn't been telling him the truth. Or at the very least, the whole truth.

Cursing himself and Bonner, he picked up the envelope and pulled out Dixie Bonner's most recent credit card records. It amazed him what money could buy. Confidential records being probably the least of it.

Shoving away thoughts of Beauregard Bonner, he concentrated on the records. If Dixie wanted her kidnapping to appear real, why would she use and sign her own credit cards?

Unless someone was forcing her to use them.

He focused on the charges for a moment. They made no sense. No car needed gas as often as she'd used her cards. Unless she was crazy—or stupid—she had to know she was leaving a trail any fool could follow.

According to this, Dixie had bought gas at the most southeastern part of the state, then begun what appeared to be a zigzag path across Montana.

Beauregard let out a bark, startling him. He looked up from the report to see the dog staring at him, recrimination in those big brown eyes now.

"Sorry." He tossed the credit card report aside and headed for the kitchen where he melted half a stick of butter in a large cast-iron skillet until it was lightly browned, then dropped in two large rib-eye steaks.

As they began to sizzle, he stabbed a big white potato a couple of times with a fork and tossed it into the microwave to cook. He considered a second vegetable but instead pulled out a Montana map and spread it out on the table. Retrieving Dixie Bonner's credit card reports, he traced a line from town to town across the state.

Alzada. Glendive. Wolf Point. Jordan. Roundup. Lewistown. Big Sandy. Fort Benton. Belt.

Chance heard the steaks sizzling and turned to see that Beauregard was keeping watch over them from his spot in front of the stove. Chance stepped to the stove to flip the steaks, opened the microwave to turn the potato, dug out sour cream, chopped up some green onions and found the bottle of steak sauce in the back of the fridge—all the time wondering what the hell Dixie Bonner's kidnappers were doing.

If there even were kidnappers.

Either way, zigzagging across Montana made no sense. Why not light somewhere? Any small Montana town would do. Or any spot in between where there was a motel or a cabin in the woods—if a person wanted to hide.

But if a person wanted to be found...

He pulled the skillet with the steaks from the burner and turned off the gas. He could hear his potato popping and hissing in the microwave.

Beauregard was licking his chops and wagging his tail. The dog watched intently as Chance cut up one of the steaks, picked up Beauregard's dish from the floor and scrapped the steak pieces into it.

"Gotta give it a minute to cool," he told the dog as he considered his latest theory.

He slapped his steak on a plate, quickly grabbed the finger-burning potato from the microwave and lobbed it onto a spot next to his steak on the plate.

Beauregard barked and raced around the cabin's small kitchen. Chance checked the dog's steak. It was cool enough.

"Merry Christmas," he said to the pooch as he set the dish on the floor. Beauregard made light work of the steak, then licked the dish clean, sliding it around the kitchen floor until he trapped it in a corner.

Chance cut a deep slit in his potato and filled it with butter, sour cream and a handful of chopped green onions as he mentally traced Dixie Bonner's path across Montana and told himself one of them was certifiable.

He took his plate to the table and ate a bite of the steak and potato, studying the map again.

Dixie wasn't trying to hide.

He'd guess she wanted to be found and she was leaving someone a message.

He frowned as he ate his dinner, trying to imagine a mind that had come up with zigzagging across the state as a way to send a message.

Then again, Dixie was a Bonner.

And unless he missed his guess, she was headed his way. He checked the map, convinced he would be seeing her soon.

Why though? He doubted she even remembered him. But he might be the only person she knew in Montana and if she was desperate enough... More than likely something else had brought her to Montana. He wondered what. Was the answer on his answering machine at his office? He swore at the thought but realized there was no getting around it. He could speculate all night or go back into town in a damned blizzard and check the machine.

As Oliver Lancaster hung up the phone, he saw a shadow move along the wall from the hallway. Quietly he stepped to the den doorway and watched his wife tiptoe at a run back up the hall.

It was comical to see, but he was in no laughing mood. Rebecca eavesdropping? He couldn't have been more shocked. Not the woman who strove to be the epitome of Southern decorum.

How much had she overheard?

He tried to remember what he'd said as he watched

her disappear around the corner. Nothing he had to fear. At least, he didn't think so.

She would just think it was business. Not that she took an interest in anything he did. He put her out of his mind. It was easy to do. Rebecca looked good and played the role of wife of the successful legal consultant for Bonner Unlimited well, but the woman was a milquetoast and banal. Too much money and too much time on her hands. She bored him to tears.

He closed the door to the study, wishing he had earlier. She'd probably heard him on the phone and decided not to disturb him. Long ago, he'd told her not to bother him with dinner party seating charts or menus. That was *her* job. He hardly saw her and that was fine with him. Fine with her, too, apparently.

Oliver cursed under his breath as he moved to the window to stare out at the darkness. Even though he knew the security system was on, the estate safe from intruders, he felt strangely vulnerable tonight. And it didn't take much to figure out why.

He prized this lifestyle, which at the center was his marriage over all else. Without Beauregard Bonner's good grace—and daughter—Oliver would be nothing but a blue blood with family name only, and he knew it.

Rebecca had all the money and that damned Beauregard, for all his country-boy, aw-shucks hick behavior, was sharp when it came to hanging on to it. Oliver had been forced to sign a prenuptial agreement. If he ever left the marriage, he'd be lucky to leave with the clothes on his back and his good name.

That meant he had to keep Rebecca happy at all costs.

Which had been easy thus far. She seemed as content as he was in their "arrangement." He left her alone and she did the same. The perfect marriage.

Nothing had changed, right?

As he started to turn from the window, he caught his reflection in the glass. He stared at himself, surprised sometimes to realize that he was aging.

He always thought of himself as he had been in his twenties. Blond, blue-eyed, handsome by any standard. A catch. Wasn't that how Rebecca had seen him? He didn't kid himself why she'd dumped Chance Walker to marry him.

Now he studied himself in the glass, frowning, noticing the fine lines around his eyes, the first strands of gray mixed in with the blond, the slightly rounded line of his jaw.

He turned away from the glass and swore. So he was aging. And yet that, too, made him feel vulnerable tonight.

He glanced around the expensively furnished room almost angrily. He wasn't giving up any of this. He'd come too far and had paid too high a price. He wouldn't go down without a fight. Especially because of Rebecca's damned dysfunctional family. Or some cowboy in Montana.

Weary at the thought, he headed upstairs hoping Rebecca was already asleep. Or at least pretending to be like she was normally. He couldn't play the loving husband. Not tonight.

THE BLIZZARD was a total whiteout by the time Chance drove back into town to his office. He'd been forced to creep along in the truck, often unable to tell where the shoulder and center line was on the highway, the falling and blowing snow obliterating everything in a blur of dense suffocating white.

His office building, when he finally reached the nearly deserted town of Townsend, Montana, was dark, all the shops closed.

He let himself in, surprised when Beauregard took off running down the hall to bark anxiously at the door to the detective agency.

Chance thought about going back to his pickup for the shotgun he carried. He hadn't carried his pistol since the last time he'd used it to kill a man, but he was almost wishing he had it as he headed down the hall.

He reminded himself that Beauregard wasn't very discriminating when it came to being protective. There could be another mouse in the office, something that had gotten the old dog worked up on more than one occasion.

Moving quickly down the hall, Chance quieted the dog and listened at the door before he unlocked his office.

Beauregard pushed open the door and streaked in the moment he heard the lock click. As Chance flipped on the light, he tensed. Beauregard Bonner's visit had him anxious. So did the dog's behavior.

He could hear the dog snuffling around his desk.

Edging into the room, Chance scanned the desktop. He could see at a glance that the papers he'd left there had been gone through.

Dixie Bonner. Was it possible she was already in town? But what could she have been looking for on his desk?

It made no sense.

Then again, little about the Bonners ever had.

Unfortunately there was no doubt that someone had been here. Just the thought made him angry.

He stepped behind the desk and checked the drawers. He didn't keep anything worth stealing, which could have been why nothing appeared to be missing.

He had a safe but it was empty. He checked to see if the intruder had found it hidden behind the print of the lower falls of the Yellowstone River he kept on the wall—the only art in the office. Moving the framed print aside, he tried to remember the safe's combination. It had been a while.

His birthday. He had to think for a moment, then turned the dial and opened the safe. Empty and untouched as far as he could tell.

Turning, he looked around the office, trying to understand why anyone would care enough to break in. He had no ongoing cases, had nothing to steal and kept any old files on CD hidden at the cabin. He didn't even leave a computer in the office, but brought his laptop back and forth from the cabin.

And maybe more to the point, anyone who knew him, knew all of this.

But Dixie Bonner didn't know him.

That's when Chance noticed the dog. Beauregard stood next to the desk, the hair standing up on the back of his neck and a low growl emitting from his throat.

Chance moved around the desk to see why the dog was acting so strangely. The desk was old. He'd picked it up at a garage sale for cheap. Because of that one of the legs was splintered. He'd had to drill a couple of screws into the oak. One screw had hit a knot and refused to go all the way in.

He stared at the head of the screw that stood out a good inch. A scrap of dark cloth clung to the screw head—a scrap of clothing that hadn't been there earlier. Just like the blood hadn't been there.

Chance took perverse satisfaction in the fact that his old desk had gotten a little bit of the intruder since, with a curse, he realized what *was* missing.

The light on the antiquated answering machine was no longer flashing and he could tell even before he opened it that the tape would be gone.

It was.

Chapter Three

Chance woke to Christmas music on the radio and sunshine. Through the window, he could see that it was one of those incredible Montana winter days when the sky is so blue it's blinding.

He could also see that it had snowed most of the night, leaving a good foot on the level. He dug out early, knowing it was going to be a long day as he cleared off the deck, then started shoveling his way to his pickup.

The moment Chance had opened the door, Beauregard bounded outside to race around in the powder. Half the time the dog had his head stuck down in it, coming up covered with snow, making Chance smile. All he could think as he shoveled was that his daughter would have loved this.

Once he had a path to the pickup, he loaded Beauregard in the front seat—against his better judgment. Sure enough, the first thing the darned dog did was shake. Snow and chunks of ice and water droplets flew everywhere.

Chance swore, brushed off his seat and climbed in after the dog. The pickup already smelled like wet dog and he knew it wasn't going to get better as he started the engine, shifted into four-wheel drive for the ride out and turned on the heater.

Beauregard, worn out by all the fun he'd been having, curled up in the corner of the seat and fell asleep instantly.

Chance turned his attention to navigating the road out of the cabin—and thinking about Dixie Bonner. Last night, after finding his office had been broken into, he'd checked his Caller ID. He recognized all but one of the calls that had come in—a long-distance number with an area code he didn't recognize. There had been eight calls from that number.

Dixie?

When he checked with the operator, she informed him that the area code was from a cell phone out of Texas. He was betting it was Dixie Bonner. But if she had a cell phone number, why hadn't her father given it to him?

He'd tried the number and got an automated voice mail. He hadn't left a message.

This morning he drove up the road far enough away from the shadow of the mountain that he figured he might be able to get cell phone service and tried the number again. Same automated voice mail.

He hung up without leaving a message and drove on up the lake to his favorite place to eat breakfast. Lake Café was at the crossroads. Anyone headed his way would have to stop at the four-way.

According to Beauregard Bonner, Dixie Bonner drove a bright red Mustang with Texas plates. Add to that a Southern accent and, no doubt, the Bonner family arrogant genes. All total, Dixie would be a woman who would stand out in a crowd. Especially a Montana one.

Chance took a booth by the window, figuring he wouldn't miss a red Mustang with Texas plates when it came by this way because he was betting he would see her before the day was out.

A radio was playing back in the kitchen. Country and western Christmas music. Another reminder that he should be at home in front of the fire, feet up, dozing on a day like this with Beauregard sprawled at his feet.

Instead he was chasing a damned Bonner.

To lighten his mood, he thought about what he would do when he had her. Christmas or no Christmas, he wasn't in a joyous let alone forgiving frame of mind. If Bonner was right about this kidnapping being bogus, then it was high time someone taught Dixie Bonner a lesson she wouldn't soon forget.

And this morning, Chance Walker felt like the man who could do it.

OLIVER WAS NOWHERE around the next morning when Rebecca woke up. She just assumed he'd gone to work already but as she came down the stairs she saw her uncle Carl heading down the hallway toward Oliver's den.

"Good morning, Rebecca." Carl was older than his brother Beauregard, about the same size but nothing like her father in nature. Carl was quiet and less driven. A whole lot less driven.

"Is Daddy here?" She couldn't help being confused. It wasn't like Carl to stop by unless there was a family dinner of some kind going on.

"I just stopped in to see Oliver," Carl said as she descended the stairs.

"Oh." Rebecca couldn't imagine what Carl would want to see her husband about. Both were employed by Bonner Unlimited, but it was no secret that neither had anything to do there.

And she knew that Carl had never approved of Oliver. She remembered when she'd announced her engagement to Oliver. Carl had taken her aside and asked her if she was sure this was what she wanted.

She'd been angry with her uncle that day and had brought up the fact that he wasn't one to give advice on relationships given that he'd never married.

"The woman I wanted was in love with someone else," was all he'd said. "I couldn't bring myself to settle for anyone else."

"Oliver is the man I want," she'd snapped.

"I just want you to be happy." He'd kissed her on the cheek and left her feeling terrible because she'd been unkind to her favorite uncle. But also, she realized now, because he'd been right to question her choice.

"Rebecca?"

She blinked.

Carl had stopped in the hallway and was studying her. "Is everything all right?"

She forced herself to smile. "Fine."

He nodded. "You have a good day, okay?" he said pleasantly as he smiled, then continued down the hall to the den.

She watched him open the den door without knocking and step in, closing it behind him. He wasn't smiling, she noticed, when he closed the door. Did this have something to do with Daddy going to Montana? Was Uncle Carl who her husband had been talking to last night on the phone?

No, she thought. More than likely he'd been on the phone with the one person who resented Daddy even more than Oliver—her father's cousin, Ace Bonner. Ace, who was Daddy's age, had recently gotten out of prison.

Daddy being Daddy, he had given Ace a job at Bonner Unlimited. She got so sick of her father feeling guilty for having so much money. He wore it like a chip on his shoulder. No matter how arrogant he came off, Beauregard Bonner didn't feel he measured up, and she hated that about him.

As she reached the bottom of the stairs, she heard raised voices, startling her. Carl never raised his voice. What had Oliver done now? Something that Carl was upset about. Let it have something to do with Bonner Unlimited, she thought. Just like Dixie being in Montana. *Just don't let it have anything to do with me.*

Rebecca had enough problems. But as she headed for the kitchen, desperately needing coffee, she couldn't shake the feeling that her world was on the verge of crumbling around her.

She found the nanny in the kitchen with the children. Amy was pounding on the high-chair tray, splashing milk everywhere. Tanya was yelling for the nanny, Ingrid, to do something about Amy. And Linsey was on her cell phone talking to her best friend Miranda.

"I'm going out," Rebecca called to Ingrid, trying to escape before the nanny took the spoon away from Amy.

As Rebecca hustled back upstairs, she shut off Amy's shrieks only after reaching her bedroom and closing the door. When the house was built, she'd had extra insulation put around their bedroom for privacy. At least that's what she told the builders.

She hadn't wanted her sleep disturbed by the children waking up in the middle of the night. That's what she had a nanny for. A light sleeper, she had to have the room a certain temperature and complete darkness. And she had the money to get exactly what she wanted.

As she climbed into the shower, she thought about her lunch date with her best friend Samantha "Pookie" Westbrook. Pookie was everything Rebecca had always wanted to be. The daughter of a well-known Houston old-money family with an impeccable reputation and the grace and charm of Texas royalty.

Imagining as she often did what her life would have been like if she'd been the Westbrook's daughter instead of Pookie, kept Rebecca from worrying about what Oliver and Uncle Carl had been arguing about in the den.

AFTER ORDERING his breakfast, Chance stepped outside to see if he could get cell phone service. It was always iffy in the mountains. He'd never been able to get a signal at the cabin, which was just fine with him.

He dug his cell out, cursing the damned thing, and on impulse, first tried the cell phone number again that had been on the Caller ID at his office. He got voice mail again and again didn't leave a message. Then he dialed the number Bonner had left for him.

"Hello?" Beauregard Bonner boomed.

"It's Chance. Any word from Dixie?" He'd been holding his breath, hoping Dixie had found her way home. Or at least there'd been some contact.

"Nothing," Bonner said. "I just flew into Houston and was going to find my other daughter."

Chance thought about telling Bonner to say hello to Rebecca, but instantly came to his senses. "Do you have a cell phone number for Dixie?"

"No. I'm sure she has one. I tried to get the number, but couldn't."

Chance smiled to himself, hearing the frustration in Bonner's voice. Even Beauregard Bonner didn't get everything he wanted.

"I'll let you know when I come up with something," Chance said and snapped the phone shut.

Back in the café, he kept an eye on the four-way stop, hoping he was right about Dixie. Of course, that brought up the question of why she was zigzagging across the state, why she was headed his way in the first place. If she even was.

All he could guess was that Dixie Bonner liked to play games—just like her father.

As Chance waited for his breakfast, he dumped the contents of the manila envelope Beauregard Bonner had given him out onto the table. Last night he'd looked at the credit card report, convinced like the police and FBI that Dixie was anything but the victim of a kidnapping.

Disgusted, he hadn't even bothered to see what else Bonner had provided him. But this morning, as the contents of the envelope spilled onto the table, a photograph fell out and he recalled that Bonner had said all he had was an older photo of Dixie.

It was a three-by-five, shot by a professional in a studio, and appeared to be Dixie Bonner's high school graduation photo.

Strange, Bonner didn't have a more recent photo of his youngest daughter. Not a snapshot taken at some birthday party, Christmas or family get-together. Chance wondered if that didn't say a lot about the Bonners and what had been going on with that family since he'd left Texas.

He stared at the young woman in the photo. Pixielike, her hair was cropped short and dyed a glaring hot pink. At the center of thick black eyeliner were two twinkling blue eyes that radiated a mischief he remembered only too well. Dixie had always been cute. The cheekbones were high and maybe her best feature. Her lips were full and turned up in a devilish grin. A hellion. Just as her father had described her.

Chance chuckled to himself thinking Dixie probably was Beauregard Bonner's comeuppance. Maybe there was justice on earth after all.

"REBECCA? *Rebecca.*"

Rebecca Bonner blinked.

"You haven't heard a word I've said," Pookie snapped irritably. They were having lunch at Rebecca's favorite restaurant. She'd hoped that lunch with her friend would improve her mood. So far it had been having the opposite effect.

"What is going on with you today?" Pookie demanded.

Rebecca shook her head, realizing this had been a mistake. She should have gone shopping instead, bought something outrageously expensive and skipped lunch. "I think I might be coming down with something."

Pookie did an eye-roll. "What is really bothering you? Is it the kids?"

It wasn't the kids. Not that Rebecca had really wanted children in the first place. It was just something you did. Like the big house, the expensive car, the clothes and the husband.

She'd had a nanny from even before she brought Linsey home from the hospital. She gave the kids little thought except when they were screaming like this morning and she had so much on her mind.

"It's not the kids."

Pookie lifted one perfectly shaped brow. "What's the bastard done now?"

"It's not Oliver, either." She sipped her strawberry daiquiri.

"Of course it is."

"Have you heard *something?*" Rebecca asked, her heart starting to pound. Pookie often knew things almost before they happened. That was one reason Rebecca had called her for lunch today. If there was a rumor going around, Rebecca wanted to be the first to hear about it and make sure it got nipped in the bud quickly.

"I haven't heard a thing." Pookie held up three fingers. As if she was ever a Girl Scout. "And I can't believe I wouldn't have heard."

Rebecca was counting on that. "You'd tell me at once if you did."

"Of course." Pookie looked worried. "Why, have you heard something about Adam?" Adam was her friend's husband. A balding, pot-bellied, thirtysomething attorney at a top agency in the city who kept Pookie in a style even better than she'd been accustomed to—which said a lot given that Pookie was born to Houston society.

"Come on, what's going on with you?" Pookie asked, leaning toward her, grinning. "Give. Who is he?"

Rebecca shook her head and tried to wave away Pookie's protests. Pookie would be surprised if Rebecca told her that she hadn't been with a man other than her husband in months. Her friend went through a lot of men and thought everyone else did, too.

"Come on. You and I have never kept secrets."

Rebecca thought how naive Pookie was. *Everyone* kept secrets. Even from their best friends if they were smart.

"I told you about my pilates instructor." Pookie pretended to pout.

"There isn't *anyone*," she said, feeling even worse. Not even Oliver. Except for that one night. He'd acted so strangely that night. She brushed the memory away, hating to remember his attempts at lovemaking. They'd never made love that she could recall. Intimacy at their house was more like a corporate takeover.

"Oliver's been acting…strange," Rebecca confided, seeing no harm in the obvious.

Pookie lifted a brow as if to ask how she could tell. "Well, if it isn't another woman…"

"He's involved in some kind of deal at work. I'm sure that's all it is. He has this thing about winning." That, she knew, was his form of orgasmic release. He had never seemed that interested in sex. Or maybe it was just her he wasn't interested in.

Pookie narrowed her eyes, studying her. "There isn't a man? Come on, I saw that look in your eye."

Rebecca groaned, knowing her friend would keep after her until she gave her something. "I was thinking about Chance Walker," she said, and braced herself for her friend's reaction.

WHEN HIS FOOD arrived—his usual—a slab of bone-in ham, two eggs over easy, hash browns and whole-wheat toast with blackberry jam, Chance placed the picture next to his plate, studying it periodically as he ate.

If he was right and the photograph was taken eleven years ago, who knew how much Dixie Bonner had changed. She was probably more outrageous than ever.

He shook his head as he thought about the kid he'd known. Would he even recognize her now?

"Girlfriend?" the waitress asked, moving for a better look at the photo.

"Not hardly. Actually, it's a case I'm working on. Any chance you've seen her? She'd be eleven years older than when this was taken."

Lydia, an older, stocky woman, shook her head. "Sorry. And believe me I would have remembered the hair if it was still that color."

"I have a feeling this one has tried it all," he said, looking at Dixie's photo.

"You sound like you know her."

"Used to, when she was twelve," he said with an amused shake of his head. "She was hell on wheels back then. I just assumed she would grow up and be more like her sister."

Lydia raised a brow.

"I dated her older sister." It surprised him the regret he heard in his voice. Not that he hadn't married Rebecca. Just that things had ended so badly.

"First love?"

"I guess it was. She went away to college back east and met someone..." Someone more appropriate. "I hear she has three kids now and her husband is a hotshot attorney in Houston."

Lydia put a hand on his shoulder. "Honey, something tells me you are better off without her."

Chance laughed. "I have no doubt about that."

"Want the rest of that ham wrapped up for Beauregard?" she asked as she cleared his table.

"Please." He put everything back in the manila envelope, including Dixie's picture, finished his coffee and took the envelope and foil-wrapped ham out to the pickup.

Beauregard devoured the ham in one bite and waited for more as Chance started the pickup. "Sorry, bud, that's it until dinner."

Taking out the map of Montana, he stared at the jagged line he'd drawn on it last night as he'd traced Dixie Bonner's route.

Dixie hadn't come to him, so that meant he'd have to go to her. If he was right, there was a definite pattern to her movements. She was headed his way. All he could figure was that she didn't want anyone to know it.

Chance found that pretty humorous since someone

obviously knew and had gone to some trouble to break into his office to take his answering machine tape. He wondered what message she'd left and why it was important to whoever was apparently looking for her.

He planned to ask her when he saw her.

There was also the remote possibility that she really had been kidnapped, that the kidnapper had foolishly left eight messages on his machine. But that brought up the question of why call him? Also, what kidnapper would leave eight messages on his machine?

He figured no matter what was going on, Dixie wouldn't have left her location or where she was headed on his answering machine. And neither would her kidnappers.

Chance swore and headed down the lake and eventually into town, figuring she should be here today if she continued her traveling pattern. The day was brilliant, the sky a deep blue, the mountains glistening white, the sun blinding overhead.

He glanced in his rearview mirror and saw a light-colored panel van pull out behind him.

"YOU WERE THINKING about Chance *Walker?*" Pookie cried, then ducked her head as several of the nearby diners frowned over at her. *"Why?"* she asked in a hushed whisper. "It wasn't like you were ever serious about him. Marrying him would have been social suicide."

Rebecca nodded. All true. She hadn't even considered *marrying* Chance. But what she hadn't told Pookie was that she'd thought he would stay around Houston. She would have had an affair with him in a heartbeat.

She'd never dreamed Chance would go to Montana to work for the summer and not return to Texas. One of the secrets she'd never told Pookie was about the breakup. Pookie had always assumed that Rebecca had broken it off with Chance because she'd met Oliver and he was the better catch hands down.

What Pookie didn't know and never would was that Chance had been the one to break off their relationship. He'd figured out that she'd never planned to marry him. Oliver knew she'd been dumped and had never let her forget it. The bastard.

So even if Chance had stayed around Houston, she doubted he would have been up for an affair. Just the thought made her angry and upset.

And now her sister was in Montana.

With Chance?

The thought killed her appetite.

"Why are you even thinking about Chance at this late date?" Pookie demanded quietly.

"I wasn't. It's just that I think Daddy is in Montana and it made me think of Chance." At least she assumed that was the "son of a bitch" Oliver had been referring to, and Oliver had said something about Dixie.

Pookie started to say something, then stopped as she looked past Rebecca and smiled. "Well, he's not in Montana anymore," she said under her breath as Rebecca heard someone approach the table from behind her.

IN HIS REARVIEW mirror Chance watched the van coming up the road behind him. The two-lane highway ran along the lake, over the dam, then headed south to Townsend where his office was located. This time of year, the road got little traffic with most of the places on the lake closed up for the winter.

Chance slowed to give the driver of the van the opportunity to pass. The van slowed, as well, staying right with him, and confirming his suspicions.

As the road began to snake around the north end of the lake, Chance sped up. The van sped up, too, the driver doing his best to stay with him, even taking some dangerous curves too fast, leaving little doubt that the driver was determined not to lose him.

Fortunately this morning there was no other traffic on the road. As Chance came around a corner with a nice wide deep ditch on each side, he braked, coming to a stop, blocking both lanes.

The van came flying around the corner. The driver hit his brakes but clearly realized there was no way he could stop on the snow-packed road and aimed the van for the ditch.

Chance pulled his pickup over to the side of the road and, taking the shotgun from the rack behind the pickup seat, jumped out to bound down into the snowy ditch to jerk open the driver's side door.

He shoved the shotgun in the man's face. "Why the hell are you following me?"

"Easy," the man cried, throwing his hands up. "I'm a private eye. Just like you."

Chance swore at the man's thick Texas drawl. "Who the hell are you?"

"Let me reach into my jacket..."

"No way." Chance reached in and withdrew the man's wallet—and a 9 mm pistol. He chucked the pistol over the top of the van where it disappeared in the deep snow. The wallet he flipped open to the man's ID. J. B. Jamison, Private Investigator, Houston Texas.

"Who hired you?" Chance asked as he tossed the wallet into the back of the empty van. Not that he didn't already know the answer.

"Bonner. Beauregard Bonner."

"What the hell did he hire you to do?" Chance demanded. "Follow *me?*"

"Find his daughter and take her back to Texas."

Chance was still pointing the shotgun at the man. "And that has what to do with me?"

"Bonner told us she might contact you."

So that was it. Beauregard was covering his bets. Setting Chance up because he thought Dixie would come to him. But lacking faith that Chance could get Dixie back to Texas. Now why was that?

"So you broke into my office and stole my answering machine tape," Chance accused.

The man looked genuinely surprised. "No. I was just tailing you, hoping you'd lead me to Ms. Bonner. That's all."

"Roll up your pant legs," Chance ordered. "Whoever broke into my office scraped his leg on my desk."

Jamison didn't look happy about it, but he pulled up one pant leg, then the other. No sign he'd been the one to get hung up on the desk.

"Get out."

Jamison looked out at the deep snow, then at Chance

and the shotgun. "I didn't break into your office. There is no reason to—"

"Out." Chance stepped back so the Texas P.I. could get out of the van. The man stepped gingerly into the deep snow. He wore loafers and slacks, although he'd been smart enough to get himself a down coat.

Chance quickly frisked the man, found no other weapon and ordered Jamison to walk out a dozen yards, through the snow and trees, from the van.

While the man's back was turned, Chance threw the van's keys into the snow and searched the van.

No answering machine tape. But what Chance did find shocked him. In the back of the van was everything a man would need to hog-tie and bind a woman to transport her back to Texas.

He felt sick as he left J. B. Jamison cursing him to hell beside the road and drove off. That bastard Bonner hadn't mentioned he put another P.I. on the case let alone that he'd sent the man to bring Dixie back to Texas.

Chance's job was to find Dixie. Period.

Under most circumstances, Chance would have quit right there. But after what he'd seen in the back of Jamison's van, he was afraid for Dixie Bonner and even more anxious to find her.

Chapter Four

Rebecca froze as she felt her father come up to her table from behind her.

"Well, look who it is," Pookie gushed. "My favorite man. I hope you're planning to join us." Pookie had the irritating habit of flirting with older men. Especially the ones with money and few had more money than Daddy. Her friend rose demurely to plant a kiss on Beauregard's check.

"You are a sinful woman," Daddy said to Pookie, but clearly enjoyed the attention. "Rebecca," he said with a nod as he stepped around to face her. She hadn't moved, hadn't said a word.

She and her father rarely spoke. He never seemed to know what to say to her. He could talk for hours with Dixie. But then, Dixie was his favorite, no matter what he said. Oh, he tried to make Rebecca feel loved. That was the problem. He tried too hard, as if it didn't come naturally the way it did with Dixie.

"What brings you into town?" Rebecca asked as sweetly as she could while pasting a smile on her face.

"Are you meeting someone?" she added, looking around the restaurant expectantly, all the time hoping he was.

"Samantha, honey, could you excuse us for a moment?"

Pookie gave Rebecca a curious look. "Of course. I'll just go powder my nose."

Beauregard Bonner took a seat across from his daughter and she saw that he was upset. She braced herself, afraid suddenly of what he was going to tell her.

"Have you seen your sister?" he asked.

She blinked, so taken off guard that she wasn't even sure she'd heard him correctly. "I beg your pardon?"

"Your sister. Dixie. You might remember her from last Christmas? No, that's right, you went back east for Christmas."

She didn't like his tone. "I remember my sister," she said coldly. He always blamed her that she and Dixie weren't closer. She was the oldest, he'd say, as if that made a difference.

"I believe you missed Christmas, as well," she shot back. "Jamaica, wasn't it? What was her name? Carmella? Lupita? I lose track."

Her father didn't seem to hear. He was trying to get the waiter's attention, no doubt for a drink.

She couldn't care less about last Christmas. Or the one before it. They'd never been that kind of family. They might have been, if her mother had lived. But she hadn't.

"What has Dixie done now?" She tried to sound bored by this conversation, but her heart was pounding. What *had* Dixie done?

"Have you talked to her lately?" he asked.

She frowned. "No, Daddy, I haven't. How about you?"

"She's…missing."

Rebecca laughed, politely of course, since they were in one of Houston's most elite restaurants. Another reason she really didn't want to have a discussion about her sister here, now.

"She's *always*…missing. I really don't see what that has to do with me." Rebecca picked up her bag from the chair next to her and started to rise. "I'm sorry, Daddy, but I really must get going. Please give my apologies to Pookie."

"Sit down." He hadn't raised his voice, fortunately. But she knew by his tone that he could at any moment. He had no compunction against making scenes. In fact, he seemed to enjoy them as if he never wanted to forget his poor white-trash roots. As he was fond of saying, "If Houston society don't like it, they can kiss my cherry-red ass."

She sat back down.

"I think she might have been kidnapped," he said quietly, and picked up her water glass and downed it. "How do you get a drink in this place?"

Rebecca caught the waiter's eye and mouthed Scotch neat. She didn't have to tell the waiter to make it the best they carried. That was a given.

"What makes you think she's been kidnapped?" she asked carefully. Bringing up Dixie's other shenanigans would only set her father off, although she would have loved to have listed them chapter and verse.

"I got a call." The waiter set down the drink and Beauregard snatched it up, downing it in two gulps before motioning for the waiter to bring him another.

"You don't seem all that upset about it," he said a little too loudly.

"Because I don't believe it," she said, keeping her voice low by example. She could always depend on her father to embarrass her. Oh, why couldn't she have come from old money like Pookie and her other friends?

"The ransom demand is a million dollars."

She stared at him. "You can't be serious?"

He gave her a deadpan look.

"How silly of me. It's *Dixie*. It is only a matter of time before she'll want it all for some foolish cause of hers." And Daddy will give it to her, Rebecca thought angrily. Oliver had warned her that Dixie would get everything in the end, hadn't he? "So you paid it. What's the problem?"

"Hell no, I didn't pay it."

The waiter set down another drink and looked nervously at Beauregard as if, like Rebecca, afraid he might be a problem.

Rebecca watched her father take one gulp. "You haven't paid it yet?" This did surprise her.

"I'm *not* paying it."

He would. Eventually. He always caved when it came to Dixie. "So what *are* you doing?"

"Obviously trying to find her."

Rebecca glanced around the restaurant. "If you'd called, I could have told you she wasn't here, Daddy."

His eyes narrowed. "Why do you have to be such a bitch?"

His words stung more than she thought they would. She knew he was only striking out because he was worried about his *other* daughter. "Why do you have to be such an ass?" she hissed back at him.

He gripped his glass, anger in every movement as he downed the last of it, and carefully put it down.

She knew she'd gone too far. But she was sick of being the other daughter. The one her father never gave a concern to. "I heard you went to Montana." She waited, hoping he would deny it.

"Who told you I went to Montana?"

She stared at her father. "You really *did* go?" She hadn't meant to sound so shocked. But she was. So she'd been right about the "son of a bitch" Oliver had been referring to.

"Isn't that what you just— Never mind," he said, and motioned to the waiter for another drink. "That's where I guess she is."

This was all too surreal, especially on top of the two strawberry daiquiris she'd consumed—and what little she'd gleaned from Oliver's phone conversation she'd overhead last night.

"I hired your old boyfriend to find her."

There it was. She hadn't been mistaken. She felt light-headed. For an instant she thought about pretending ignorance and saying, "What boyfriend would that be, Daddy?"

Instead she said, "You hired Chance Walker to find Dixie?" saying his name carefully as if the words were expensive crystal that were so fragile they might break otherwise.

"He's a private detective. Damned good."

Was that supposed to make her feel better?

Daddy was looking at her, studying her, his eyes glazed from the alcohol, but he wasn't drunk. Nor was he stupid. "You were a fool not to marry him."

"I beg your pardon?"

He picked up the fresh drink the waiter left on the table and stared down into it as if it were more fascinating than her by far.

"I beg your pardon?" she said again, leaning toward him over the table, working to keep her voice down. After all, she was part of this family and no stranger to loud, ugly scenes. Just not in public.

"You, of all people, *know* why I married Oliver," she said, her voice low and crackling with fury. "To give this family respectability because even with all your money, Daddy, you couldn't buy it, could you?"

He didn't look at her, but what she saw on his face shocked her. Shame.

She felt sick. He'd known what she'd done and why. He'd never believed that she married Oliver for love. He'd known that she had sacrificed her own happiness for the family and he hadn't even tried to stop her.

She rose from the table, picking up her purse, glaring down at him. "As I said, I have things to do." She turned on her heel.

Just as he hadn't stopped her from marrying Oliver, he didn't stop her from leaving the restaurant.

CHANCE DROVE DOWN the road to where a wide spot had been plowed at the edge of the lake and pulled over. He tried to calm down before he called Bonner again.

"Hello?" Bonner sounded asleep. Or half-drunk.

Because of the hour and the bar sounds in the background, Chance surmised it was the latter.

"What the hell are you trying to pull?" He'd planned to be calm, not to tell Bonner what he thought of him. But just the sound of the oilman's voice set Chance off.

"Chance?"

"I just met the private eye you hired from Texas. J. B. Jamison. Want to tell me what the hell that was about?"

"I don't know what you're talking about."

"A Texas private investigator named J. B. Jamison."

"He said *I* hired him? Well, he's mistaken. You're the only private investigator I hired."

Chance swore. "Mistaken? How could he mistake that?"

"Maybe someone hired him using my name, but it wasn't me," Bonner snapped. "I give you my word."

For what that was worth. It was all he could do not to tell Bonner what he thought of that. Instead, Chance thought of his own daughter.

"Someone broke into my office last night," Chance said. "From what I can tell, it wasn't Jamison. That means there is someone else looking for Dixie."

"Well, I didn't hire them," Bonner said, sounding angry. "How many times do I have to say it?"

Chance shook his head, fighting to rein in his temper. If not Jamison, then who had broken into the office and taken the answering machine tape?

"Let's be clear on this," Chance said. "I'll find your daughter. That's what you're paying me to do. I'll even give her a ride to the airport so she can return to Houston, if that's what she wants. But I won't let anyone use the kinds of methods Jamison does and hog-tie her and haul her across state lines all the way back to Texas. *That's* kidnapping and I won't be a part of it no matter what's going on between you and Dixie."

He heard Bonner take a long drink. Glasses tinkled in the background, the clatter of dishes, the murmur of people talking. The bastard was having lunch.

"Just find my daughter as quickly as possible. I got another ransom demand. A million and a half. There was also a package waiting for me at the airport when I landed. Dixie's locket was inside it. It's the one I gave her on her sixteenth birthday. She wore it all the time."

Chance groaned. "Damn it, Beauregard. Call the FBI. They can start tracing the calls."

Beauregard the dog lifted his head, coming awake at the sound of his name—and Chance's angry tone.

"We've already had this discussion," Bonner said, sounding tired. "She used her credit card again. Some place called Neihart, Montana? Call me the minute you have her. But I warn you, finding her and hanging on to her are two entirely different things. By the time you're done, you'll understand why this Jamison uses the methods he does." Bonner hung up.

Chance snapped off the phone with a curse. What the hell? Bonner sounded as if he still didn't believe his daughter had been kidnapped. But he was worried about her. What was going on?

Beauregard the dog barked, letting him know he didn't appreciate being awakened by Chance's raised voice when he'd done nothing wrong.

"Go back to sleep. I'll wake you for lunch." Chance

patted the dog's big head and Beauregard curled back up, dropping off to sleep again instantly. Dogs. They really did have the life.

Every instinct told Chance to call the oilman back and quit the case. Unfortunately it had gone beyond the money. Chance couldn't let Jamison find Dixie first. No matter what a hellion the woman was. Someone had damned sure hired Jamison to haul her back to Texas. But why?

Bonner wasn't going to the feds because whatever was really going on, he didn't want them involved. What the hell had Dixie done? Whatever it was, Bonner just wanted her quietly returned to the longhorn state. Illegally returned, since Dixie was twenty-nine.

Why wasn't Bonner worried that his daughter would press charges against him once he got her back to Texas?

Another good question.

He dragged out his map again. If he was reading her traveling pattern right, she was headed for White Sulphur Springs.

He couldn't wait any longer. It was time to cut her off at the pass.

ACE BONNER was leaning against Oliver's Porsche, grinning as Oliver came out of the Bonner Unlimited building. Ace was a big fifty-something man with thick gray hair. He'd probably been fairly good-looking, like most of the Bonners, when he was younger. But prison and an indulgent lifestyle since hadn't done much for him.

"What are you doing here?" Oliver snapped as he glanced back at the Bonner Unlimited building, afraid Carl or Mason might be watching them from the window.

"Cool your jets," Ace said, putting his arm around Oliver's shoulder. "Hell, we're family. Nothing wrong with the two of us being seen together."

"There is when we have a deal going down," Oliver said under his breath as he shrugged off Ace's arm and walked around to the driver's side, hoping to make a fast exit. "And stay off my car."

"We need to talk," Ace said, the grin gone.

Oliver looked at him. "What? Something to do with the deal?"

"I need to grease another wheel." He raised his hands before Oliver could protest. "It's almost a done deal. Just this one guy who could hold things up. No reason to get cheap now."

"Except that I don't have it," Oliver snapped.

Ace cocked his head at him. "Don't give me that crap, Lancaster." His gaze went to the car. "What's another twenty-five grand to you?"

"Twenty-five grand." He choked on the words.

"I promise that will be the last of it. Hell, we're in a position to make six mil. You're going to bitch about twenty-five lousy grand?"

Oliver glared at Ace, too angry to speak. "If this deal doesn't go through and I find out that it was all a scam—"

"Please. I'm going to blow three million dollars for the measly hundred grand you've given me for the deal?"

"Two."

"Two what?"

"Two hundred thousand dollars," Oliver said, elongating each word.

"You want me to swing by your house and pick up the money?" Ace asked.

"No." He hadn't meant the word to come out so sharply. "I'll contact you when I get it."

"Right," Ace said, grinning, but there was a sour look in his eyes that Oliver didn't like. Once this deal went through Oliver was going to put as much distance as he could between himself and Ace Bonner.

As Chance drove into White Sulphur Springs, he watched for Dixie's red Mustang. He couldn't imagine the kidnapper driving it. Or Dixie, for that matter. If she didn't want to be found, she would have ditched it for something less noticeable. Even if the kidnapping was bogus, by now she had to have realized that people were looking for her.

Chance told himself that this could be nothing more sinister than a power struggle between father and daughter. Bonner was definitely stubborn enough. And probably Dixie, too, from the sounds of it. Maybe Chance was overreacting. Maybe she wasn't in any kind of trouble. Her father, either.

But still, Chance couldn't shake the feeling that Bonner sincerely was afraid for his daughter. And with good reason.

Chance drove down the main drag, then started down side streets, wondering if he wasn't nuts. This felt like a wild-goose chase. Maybe there was no rhyme or reason for Dixie to zigzag across the state. No message. No game plan.

But as he was driving past a house known in these

parts as the Castle, he saw something that made him pull up short.

When the Castle had been built in 1892, it was a stone mansion constructed out of local carved granite. The story was that the house had been built for the owner's soon-to-be wife, with no expense spared, including a bathtub.

As Chance remembered the story, the marriage didn't work out, bathtub and all. The Castle was now a museum. The story of past disappointments seemed to fit given that parked behind it was a bright red Mustang with Texas plates.

Chance pulled his pickup over across the street from the Castle and stared at the woman standing out front. No one else was around, the museum apparently closed.

He'd thought he wouldn't recognize her. Not after this many years. Dixie had looked nothing like her sister Rebecca. Rebecca had been petite and dainty, her blond hair a sleek cap that framed her perfect face.

This woman standing in front of the museum was as long-legged as a colt, and she was wearing a pair of form-fitting jeans that hugged her derriere. She had a slim waist that tapered up to nice broad shoulders that were only partially hidden by a wild dark mane of long curly hair.

The last time he'd seen Dixie Bonner she'd been twelve. Not even filled out. But she'd been tall for her age, slim and had this wild, dark, curly long hair...

He opened his pickup door and stepped out. She didn't turn as he started across the street, but he had the distinct impression that she knew he was here although she still seemed intent on studying the museum hours. Definitely not acting like a woman who'd been kidnapped or who feared for her life. More like a woman who had nothing more on her mind than a vacation.

The squeal of tires and the growl of an engine startled him. He turned in time to see a large black sedan come roaring up the street. For an instant he thought it might be teenagers acting up. But teens in these parts drove old pickups or clunker cars with primer paint and missing fenders—not what looked a whole lot like a full-size rental car.

The car came to a skidding stop in front of the museum between him and Dixie. The passenger side door flew open and a large man launched himself at Dixie.

No doubt she'd heard the car approach. She swung around almost as if she'd been expecting them. She caught the big man in the face with her shoulder bag and then kneed him in the groin. He dropped like a sack of Idaho potatoes, fell off the museum steps and into the snowbank where he floundered in pain.

The driver started to get out, but saw Chance come running across the street, gun drawn.

Horn blaring, the driver hit the gas, almost leaving his passenger who, covered with snow, limped hurriedly after the car. The big man barely managed to get in before the driver gunned the engine, the tires squealing as the car took the first corner and disappeared.

"Are you all right?" Chance asked, running up to her. If he'd doubted before that she was Dixie Bonner, he didn't now. Only a Bonner attracted trouble the way magnets attract tacks.

She glanced at his gun but other than that had no reaction, as if this was a daily occurrence, men trying to grab her off the street and others running up with loaded guns in their hands.

Her gaze skimmed over him. He saw he'd been wrong about her best feature. From her high school senior portrait he'd thought it was her high cheekbones. Now he couldn't decide if it was her big blue eyes fringed in dark lashes or her mouth, the full lips turned up at the corners in a perfect bow.

He was about to go with the mouth when she drawled, "You certainly took your sweet time getting here, Chance Walker."

Chapter Five

"Excuse me?"

Dixie took Chance Walker in as if he were a cool drink of water. What she'd loved about him when she was twelve were the same things that Rebecca had tried to change about him. Chance had always been rough around edges.

Montana, it seemed, had made him more so. She saw that he'd aged, but wonderfully, like a good leather couch. There were fine lines around his eyes, but his brown eyes were softer somehow as if life had humbled him over the years and yet at the same time made him stronger.

"Excuse me?" he repeated with a shake of his head. "I believe 'thank you' would be the appropriate response since I just saved your scrawny behind."

"My behind is definitely *not* scrawny," she said. "And it's debatable just how much help you were."

His grin brought it all back. Chance Walker was just as Dixie had remembered him. Obstinate, arrogant and positively the best-looking man she'd ever seen at the age of twelve.

She'd had *the* worst crush on him and could still

recall the horrible ache she'd felt whenever he was around. He'd treated her like the kid she was at the time. That hadn't made it hurt any less.

"Right. That was genius the way you waited in front of a castle for them," he snapped.

She wanted to tell him how good it was to see him. Because it was. She wanted to throw herself into his arms. But at the same time she didn't want him to see how scared she was and had been for days.

She flashed him a grin that was more cocky than she felt. "I was waitin' on *you*. Nice you finally got one of my messages and figured out where I would be."

"Me, and everyone else apparently. Why didn't you just send up a flare?"

She glared at him. "I figured if I waited for you in front of a castle on the edge of town you couldn't really miss me."

He shook his head and looked down the street. "Well, unless you want to wait for those guys to come back, I suggest we hightail it out of here."

She nodded, irritated with him. She tried to relax, telling herself she had nothing to worry about now. Hadn't she known that Chance would find her? He'd been her hero when she was twelve. She'd always known that if there was one person she could trust it was Chance Walker if she ever got into any real trouble. And she was in a world of trouble.

"I thought I'd be seeing you *before* this, given the number of messages I left," she said as they started across the street. She slowed, looking over at him when he didn't answer right away.

He glanced down the street, frowning, then settled his gaze on her. "I didn't get the messages. Someone broke into my office and took the answering machine tape before I could get them. I haven't been working for a while."

She stopped dead in the middle of the street. "Then how did you know where…"

He stopped, too, looking at her as if she'd lost her mind. "We really need to get out of here. Unless I miss my guess, we'll be seeing those guys again."

"How did you find me?" She couldn't move because even before he said the words, she knew.

He sighed as he pulled off his cowboy hat and raked a hand through his thick hair. "Your father told me you were in Montana. I figured out where you were headed by tracking the credit card charges he gave me."

She stared at him, her heart sinking like the *Titanic*. "My *father?* Why would my father…" She couldn't believe this. Fear shot through her, mixed with equal amounts of anger and disappointment. "No. You wouldn't."

He rocked back, seemingly surprised by her reaction. "Could we talk about this somewhere else besides the middle of the street?"

She felt her car keys in her coat pocket and glanced toward the back of the museum, gauging whether or not she could reach her car before he caught her.

It wasn't her anger that brought the hot stinging tears to her eyes but the betrayal. She would have trusted Chance with her life. *Had.* She'd stupidly contacted him believing he was the one person who couldn't be bought by her father.

"What is my father paying you to do?" she asked, trying to keep her voice steady.

He was looking at her closely now, a wariness in his gaze. She knew he'd seen her anger—as well as her tears. He didn't even try to deny that her father had hired him. "Look, clearly you're in trouble. I just want to help you."

She laughed and looked away, biting at her lower lip, still considering making a run for it. "If you're working for my father then you aren't here to help me." She met his gaze. "What did he pay you to do? Stop me?"

"He just wants you to come back to Texas. He's afraid for you. But I would imagine you know more about that than I do."

She stared at the man she'd measured all men by since she was twelve. "You bastard." She turned and took off at a dead run for her car.

Chance couldn't believe it. He tore off after her. She was fast, all legs, but he caught her before she reached the curb. Grabbing her arm, he spun her around to face him.

"What the hell is wrong with you?" he demanded, holding her shoulders in his palms.

"What the hell is wrong with *you?*" she snapped instantly, anger flashing like lightning in all that blue. Her voice was deeper than her sister's. This was no mealy-mouthed, soft-spoken Southern belle. This woman had attitude, as well as backbone. She was a firecracker, hotheaded and sharp-tongued. A real handful—just as her father had warned him.

He should have known that the unmanageable,

stubborn, too-smart-for-her-britches girl he'd known at twelve would grow into this fiery to-be-reckoned-with woman.

In answer, she swung that shoulder bag, to cuff him the way she had the other poor sucker, but he'd been expecting it. He caught the bag and blocked her next move, not interested in being kneed in the groin or ending up in a snowbank.

"Damn it, I'm trying to help you. Why can't you believe that?" he said, holding on to both of her arms and keeping her at a safe distance from his groin.

"Because you were bought by my father, just like the rest of them." She spit the words at him, her eyes narrowed to slits. He could feel the anger coursing through her body and feared if he let go of her, she would launch herself at him again. They were wasting valuable time arguing on the street like this.

"I wasn't bought by *anyone*. Especially Beauregard Bonner. Don't you know me better than that?"

"I *thought* I did."

"Look, whatever this is between you and your father, I don't care, okay? I want to help, starting with getting us both out of here." He gave her arms a little tug. "Come on." He thought she'd fight him. But somewhere in the distance came the roar of an engine.

He watched her face, trying to read her expression. Fear? Or something else?

She didn't look happy about it but she let him hustle her across the street to his pickup.

Fortunately with the holidays so close, this part of town was pretty deserted with people either at work or shopping. They reached the truck without incidence, but Chance had a bad feeling it wasn't going to last.

"Where are you taking me?" She sounded suspicious and worried as she walked around to the passenger side of the truck.

"Somewhere safe." He waited for her to open her door and get in, half expecting her to try to take off again. He remembered what Bonner had said about "keeping" Dixie once he found her.

"What about my car?" she asked, looking back toward the museum.

"We'll come back for it." What he really meant was that he'd see that it got back to Texas. "Get in." He planned to get this job done and enjoy Christmas, come hell or Dixie Bonner.

She opened the pickup door and he did the same on his side. They looked at each other across the bench seat over Beauregard the dog who was sprawled like a lumpy blanket on the floor under the steering wheel out of Dixie's sight.

Her gaze, a mind-blowing blue, locked with his and he thought he glimpsed an instant of vulnerability. She still had a light sprinkling of freckles across those high cheekbones that she'd had at twelve, but on her they were now nothing short of sexy.

Any man looking into that face would have melted on the spot.

Unless that man had known the twelve-year-old Dixie Bonner and had an inkling of what she was capable of.

Or unless that man was Chance Walker and incredibly suspicious of everything—and everyone—by nature. Especially Dixie Bonner.

"You have to believe me, Chance," she said, her eyes locked with his, but still not getting into the pickup. Waiting for him to say he believed whatever she was going to say? Or stalling for time so that car with the two guys would have a chance to come back?

He couldn't help but think that the scene he'd just witnessed had been set up just for him. If Dixie wanted him to believe she was in danger, why not set it up so two big guys try to abduct you at the same time dumb ol' Chance Walker shows up?

It was that damned suspicious nature of his.

But added to what Bonner had told him about his youngest daughter—and what Chance himself already knew, he wouldn't put anything past her.

"We can talk about this in the truck," he said.

"Someone's trying to kill me." Those big baby blues misted over. She bit her lower lip, then looked away as if embarrassed by her moment of weakness.

He felt a strong tug at his heartstrings, then had to remind himself again who he was dealing with. But until he had her in the pickup… "Who's trying to kill you? The guys in the car?"

She said nothing as she looked down the street and blinked back tears.

"How *many* people are after you?" He hadn't meant it to sound so flip. "Come on, get in the truck. We need to get going. You can tell me all about it."

He saw her hesitate, then finally acquiesce. Swearing

under his breath, he started to climb behind the wheel. Was she serious? Crazy? Lying? All of the above?

Dixie stepped up on the running board to climb in and let out a surprised sound when she finally saw the dog come up off the floor. "What is it?"

"A *dog*."

She mugged a face at Chance. "I can see that. What kind?"

"Heinz 57 varieties. Just like me."

She eyed him. "Just like a lot of people. Does he bite?"

"Only people who piss me off."

She smiled faintly. "Then I guess I've been warned."

"Scoot over, Beauregard, and let her in," Chance said, dragging the dog over to give her more room.

"You named your dog *Beauregard?*"

It was Chance's turn to smile. "That's exactly what your daddy said."

"I bet he did." Beauregard grudgingly curled in the middle of the bench seat and Dixie climbed in, her nose wrinkling at the smell of damp dog. Beauregard sniffed her hand then settled himself and went back to sleep.

"Damp dog your normal cologne? Bet you don't date much," Dixie said as she slammed the pickup door and he started the engine, muttering under his breath.

At least they were on a familiar level. She'd been a smart-mouthed kid at twelve, always giving him a hard time. And vice versa.

Out of the corner of his eye, he watched her relax a little as she leaned back in the seat and gazed out at the mountains. It surprised him, but he realized that he'd missed her smart mouth. He shook his head at the thought. He hadn't missed her older sister Rebecca and that seemed a terrible thing given that she really had been his first love.

He turned his thoughts back to the problem at hand as he skirted town, debating where to take her. The obvious thing to do was to head back the way he'd come. But that would no doubt involve running into J. B. Jamison. And there was also whoever had broken into his office.

Clearly, someone after her knew about him and would expect him to return to his office in Townsend. But why take the answering machine tape? Just to find Dixie? Or to keep her from telling him something?

That last thought struck a chord.

He warned himself not to get any more involved. He'd found Dixie. All he had to do was to give Bonner a call. His job would be over and he could get back to enjoying the holidays like he'd planned.

"I'm serious, Chance. I left Texas because someone is trying to kill me," she said, not looking at him.

"What did you do in Texas to make someone want to kill you?" he asked, only half joking.

She glanced over at him, a thin smile curling that amazing mouth of hers. Who would have ever thought that Rebecca's kid sister would grow into such a stunning woman? It was that combination of big blue eyes, wide, bow-shaped mouth and high cheekbones. Not to mention that it was framed by wild dark hair that shone in the sunlight streaming in the pickup windows. She had the kind of face you couldn't help staring at.

"What did my father tell you about me?" she asked.

He could feel those blue eyes on him. "Not much. Just that you're a hellion. That you've kidnapped yourself a few times. That the ransom demand has been going up steadily since you were three."

"That's *all?*" she asked.

"There's *more?*" Of course there was more or they wouldn't be here now.

"Aren't you curious why my father is so intent on getting me back to Texas?"

Hell yes, he was. He pulled up to a stop sign and looked over at her. "I don't get paid to be curious." Which just happened to be true. But he also knew that getting curious about Dixie Bonner would lead to nothing but trouble.

"Look, if you'll just take me back to my car—"

"I can't do that."

"I beg your pardon?"

He met her gaze. "Your father hired me to make sure you were safe. Clearly you wouldn't be safe back at your car."

Her face reddened with anger. "I'm twenty-nine years old. If you try to take me back to Texas, I will have you arrested for kidnapping."

He laughed. "You can't have it both ways. Do you really believe the cops or the feds are going to believe that you've been kidnapped? They've already written off your latest attempt to extort money from your father as just that."

She stared at him. "What are you talking about?"

"The million dollars you were demanding for ransom. Excuse me, I guess it's gone up to a mil and a half now."

"I don't have any idea what you're talking about."

He stared into that face. He wanted to believe her. He really did. But then he wanted to believe anything that came out of that mouth.

"I'm talking about those guys back there," he said, getting angry. "You set up that whole show, the Castle in the background, two guys driving up just when I did, you managing to fight them off. Come on, admit it. This is just some game you and your father are playing."

She looked away. "I heard you were a pretty good private investigator."

The "pretty good" rankled even though that was pretty much how he would have described himself.

She swung around to face him, eyes piercing him like laser beams. "If you think this is a game, then you're a lousy P.I. and an even worse judge of character. But then again, you *are* working for my father, aren't you?"

Chance swore. Hadn't he known that getting involved with the Bonners was like sticking his hand into a wasps' nest hoping he wouldn't get stung?

She reached for the pickup's door handle but he reached faster, his hand clamping down on her arm as he leaned over the dog.

"I don't know what you're trying to pull, but it isn't going to work on me. So why don't you try being straight with me?"

Even if her blue eyes hadn't been snapping with anger, he could feel her rage under his fingertips where they gripped her arm.

"I didn't kidnap myself. I never made a ransom

demand. Whether you believe it or not, my life is in danger."

He didn't believe it and it must have shown because she jerked free of his grip. But she didn't try to get out of the pickup as he drove on through the intersection and headed north out of town.

He was going the wrong way to get back to Townsend.

But he didn't care because whether he liked it or not, he needed to know what he was dealing with before he went any further.

Dixie was frowning, chewing on her lower lip, eyes angry slits. But there was also a hurt in her expression that bothered him like a sliver just under his skin.

What if she was telling the truth?

He reminded himself that lying ran in some families like freckles or high cheekbones. Dixie Bonner came by her lying genes honestly enough. And Bonner had gotten proof from the kidnappers. "The kidnappers mailed your father your locket."

Her hand went to her throat. She seemed surprised to find her locket gone. Or was that, too, part of the act?

"You telling me someone took it from around your neck without you knowing about it?" he asked, unable to keep the sarcasm out of his voice.

"I would imagine they took it while I was knocked out after they abducted me in Texas. I've been a little too distracted to have noticed since then."

He turned to stare at her. "You were abducted in Texas and brought to Montana?"

"Not exactly."

He groaned inwardly, still debating the best place to

take her as she told him a story of being attacked in a parking garage in Houston, knocked out, waking up in the trunk of her car in her garage to hear the men ransacking her house, and then miraculously getting away.

"Wow, that's some story," was all he could say when she finished. He felt her gaze on him and looked over to see her big baby blues brimming in tears.

She made an angry swipe at them. "Damn you, what about that don't you believe?"

He didn't know where to start. Surely Bonner had gone to check his daughter's house. Wouldn't he have mentioned if the house had been ransacked? "So how exactly did you get away?"

She eyed him as if she thought he was just humoring her. And when he thought she wasn't going to tell him, she changed her mind and did.

He listened as she told a harrowing tale of how she had narrowly escaped from the trunk, leaving him torn between disbelief and distress at the thought that this really could have happened to her.

"I didn't know what to do. I just knew I had to get out of Texas. I needed help, but mostly I needed someone I could trust." She let out a sarcastic laugh.

He shot her a look, thinking that was pretty sad if true. Was there really no one in Texas she felt she could trust to help her? At the same time, he was touched that she'd come to him. Just as it made him suspicious of her motives.

She glanced out the side window, turning quickly back his way and sliding down a little in her seat.

Past her, he caught sight of a dark gray SUV at a side

street. Had she thought it was the black car for a minute? Is that why she'd reacted the way she had?

He took the road out of town and saw her glance back then sit up a little straighter. In his rearview mirror, he saw that there was no one behind them as they left White Sulphur Springs. No dark gray SUV.

He glanced at Dixie, unable to shake the feeling there was more she was keeping from him. "Wouldn't most women have gone to the police the moment they escaped?"

"I don't know what most women would have done," Dixie said, an edge to her voice. "I'm not *most* women. I'm the daughter of Beauregard Bonner, remember? That comes with its own rule book. I just know what *I* did under those circumstances."

He said nothing.

"Obviously you have no idea how much power my father now wields in Texas," she said. "And it seems his power extends all the way to Montana, given how easily he bought you."

Chance ground his teeth, checked his rearview mirror—and let out a curse as he spotted a car coming up way too fast behind them. The dark gray SUV.

Chapter Six

Mason Roberts was waiting for Beau in his office. As Beau stepped in and closed the door, Mason turned from where he stood at the window looking out.

"You have the best view in the entire building," he said in answer to Beau's unasked question as to what he was doing in the boss's office. Mason knew him too well, anticipating that he would come back here rather than go to that huge empty house alone.

"It's not a bad view," Bonner agreed, even though he knew the view had nothing to do with why Mason was waiting for him.

"Is everything all right?" Mason asked as he moved to the bar to make them both a drink as he always did.

Beau took a seat behind his desk. Mason had lived down the road and been like family since they were kids, both going their own ways for a while, but ending up back in Texas. Beau had offered his old friend a job and Mason, who was as smart as anyone when it came to money, had taken it.

"Why wouldn't everything be all right?" Beau asked, wondering what Mason had heard.

"Dixie?" Mason asked, turning from the bar with a glass in each hand.

Bonner took the Scotch Mason offered him. He didn't need any more to drink today but he never turned down Scotch—especially the good stuff he kept stocked in his office.

He was tired, worn out and discouraged. This wasn't the way it should have been. He was rich, damn it. He'd always thought that once he had enough money all his troubles would just fade away. Even those from the past.

"Dixie?" he repeated, pretending he didn't know what Mason was getting at.

"She up to her usual?" Mason asked.

So Mason had heard. "I'm afraid so, but I have it covered." He downed the drink, avoiding his friend's gaze as he let the alcohol warm him to his toes.

"If there's anything I can do…."

Mason had been running interference for him since they were kids. His friend seemed to be waiting for Beau to tell him what was really going on.

Not this time. "It's a family matter."

Mason winced as if Beau had hit him and Beau realized belatedly that he'd hurt his feelings. "You know what I mean. Just my daughter being Dixie." Beau put down his glass and rubbed his temples, feeling a headache coming on.

Chance would find Dixie and, with any luck, she would be flying home in time for Christmas. He would talk to her. Explain everything. Dixie was smart. She could be made to understand.

Then they would have a nice Christmas like a normal family. But even as he thought it, Beauregard Bonner knew the chance of having a normal Christmas was out of his grasp. Dixie had made certain of that.

CHANCE WATCHED THE CAR behind him coming up fast. Out of the corner of his eye, he caught Dixie's expression as she turned in her seat to look back again.

"How many people did you say were after you?" he asked as the dark gray SUV bore down on them.

Not surprisingly, she didn't answer, but he noticed that she'd slid down again in the seat as if she didn't want to be seen.

He swore, determined to get her somewhere and to get the truth out of her. More and more he was convinced the earlier scene at the museum had been staged, that the guys in the black car were in on whatever was going on and that he was a pawn in all this. So who was in the dark gray SUV?

The driver closed the distance and Chance saw what appeared to be a single occupant in the car.

He still held out hope that the driver might not even be someone interested in them at all. Maybe even someone who didn't want to run them off the road or shoot at them. Could be just some kid driving his parents' SUV too fast.

Unfortunately he'd seen the way Dixie acted after spotting the vehicle the first time. The SUV filled his rearview mirror just an instant before he heard the blare of the horn and the driver roared around him, pulling alongside as if to pass on the two-lane. But, of course, didn't.

"Get down!" Chance yelled to Dixie as he braced himself for some defensive driving if not some defensive ducking in anticipation of the barrel end of a weapon pointed in his direction.

Instead the driver was waving frantically for him to pull over.

Was the guy nuts?

The driver laid on his horn again, waving wildly and pointing—not at Chance. But at what little could be seen of Chance's passenger.

Chance shot a look at Dixie. She had slid down some more, one hand on her forehead, the other resting on Beauregard, her face turned away as if pretending this wasn't happening.

"You know this guy?" Chance demanded.

OLIVER LANCASTER was having a bad day. He'd gone to lunch after running into Ace and come back into the office hoping to find a way to get another twenty-five thousand together.

He'd cleaned out every reserve he had, including his children's college funds. Not that he wasn't going to replace the money. He had to before Rebecca found out and went postal over it. Or worse, went to her father.

This deal was taking too long. He'd gone from nervous to scared. Everything was riding on it paying off the debts he'd incurred before anyone knew about them.

But Ace needed another twenty-five thousand.

And Oliver not only didn't have it, he wasn't sure he could even scrape that much together. He'd borrowed money on everything he owned, including the house that Beau had purchased for them as a wedding present.

Oliver was starting to sweat just thinking about it. He couldn't go to Beau for the twenty-five grand. Or Carl, not after that impromptu visit from his wife's uncle this morning. Carl had come by to give him some speech about being a better husband to Rebecca. What the hell had that been about?

Like any of this was Carl's business.

But it had still scared Oliver because it must mean that even her uncle Carl had noticed that Rebecca hadn't been happy lately. Great. Oliver did not need this on top of everything else.

He'd promised Carl he'd make every effort to be a better husband. So going to Carl now for money was definitely out.

Even if Beau hadn't been in Montana, Oliver couldn't ask him for the money. As Carl had said, Beau had a lot on his mind. He was under enough stress without having to worry about Rebecca.

Carl had made him promise also not to let any problems between Oliver and his wife become something else that Beau had to worry about.

What an ass the man was.

The only reason Oliver had made the stupid promises was to get rid of the man. He'd been expecting a call from Ace and the last thing he needed was Uncle Carl getting wind of the deal he had going with Ace. Ace Bonner was the family outcast. For sure Carl wouldn't have approved of that association even if Beau was helping Ace get back on his feet.

It was odd, though. Carl had mentioned the stress Beau was under and Mason had said something about how Beau seemed to be making bad decisions, losing some of his edge, and had hinted that maybe it was time for Beau to retire as president of Bonner Unlimited and let someone…younger take over.

Since Oliver was the youngest of the bunch, he'd assumed Mason was trying to tell him something. With Beau out of the way… Well, the possibilities were unlimited.

But until then…

"I can't take this any longer," Oliver said to his empty office. He needed to get out of here, go to the club for a few drinks and try to win the twenty-five thousand. Maybe his luck would change. Hell, maybe he could win a bundle.

He touched his intercom and informed his secretary he'd be leaving for the day. But as he started around his desk he heard his private office door open.

"Oliver?"

Damn.

"Beau," Oliver said, forcing himself to sound glad to see his father-in-law. Just his luck.

"I ASKED YOU if you knew this guy?" Chance repeated as the SUV stayed right with them and the man behind the wheel continued to motion for Chance to pull over.

Dixie leaned forward to do a quick glance across the dog and him to the driver of the SUV. "He doesn't look familiar."

Chance looked over at the driver of the SUV again. The guy appeared really upset now, having seen Dixie look over at him. He was mouthing something Chance couldn't make out. But it wasn't as if the guy was trying to tell him that he had a taillight out or a tire going flat.

No, this guy was angry. And he seemed to be spewing all that venom in Dixie's direction. He hadn't tried to kill her, though. Apparently he just wanted to talk to her.

As they came around a curve, Chance looked up and swore. A semi-truck was approaching in the SUV's lane and a rancher on an old tractor was puttering along dead ahead in Chance's lane.

In a split second of insanity, Chance tromped on the gas pedal, zooming ahead of the SUV and forcing the driver to drop back behind him. With the speedometer climbing, Chance swerved between the farmer on the slow-moving tractor and the semi barreling toward him in the opposite lane.

The semi blew by with a half dozen cars backed up behind it on the two-lane an instant later.

Chance heard Dixie let out a held breath. He checked his rearview mirror. Just as he'd hoped, the SUV driver had been forced to come to a crawl behind the tractor as the semi and the line of cars passed.

Chance had bought himself a little time.

He glanced over at Dixie. She looked pale but relieved. He caught her glancing in her side mirror and chewing at her lower lip. What the hell was going on with her? He hated to venture a guess, but one thing was certain. There were definitely people after her.

But to kill her?

Or to drag her back to Houston?

Something had Dixie Bonner on the run.

What were the chances it was because of something she'd done?

"Have a minute?" It wasn't really a question as Beau closed the office door and motioned for Oliver to sit back down. Beau went straight to the bar. He made sure that even Oliver's office was stocked with his own favorite Scotch.

But to Oliver's surprise, his father-in-law poured himself a cup of coffee from the carafe left by the secretary.

Fortunately, Beau seldom came to the office and didn't seem to have any interest in the way Oliver spent his days as long as there were no problems with what little Beau let him handle. Or on the home front.

He motioned that he didn't want any coffee or a drink but Beau apparently had poured him a drink anyway. Hell, was he going to need one? Had Rebecca found out about the children's college funds? Or the other things Oliver had to mortgage?

"What's up?" Oliver asked, still standing.

"Dixie's taken off," Beau said as if this were news. He handed Oliver his usual vodka tonic and, with the coffee in hand, dropped into the deep leather chair across from Oliver's desk. Another addition Beau had made to the office for his rare visits.

"What do you mean 'taken off'?" Oliver asked as he lowered himself back into his chair, pretending this was news. And hoping it had nothing to do with him.

Beau looked him in the eye and for a moment Oliver felt as if the man was two steps ahead of him—maybe even more. "Rebecca didn't tell you?"

"I haven't spoken with her today," Oliver said. True, but an obvious mistake to tell the father-in-law just how little contact he had with the man's daughter. "We've been playing telephone tag all day."

Beau sent him a look that was equal parts disgust and disbelief. He didn't have to tell Oliver that he'd better keep Rebecca happy. But, of course, Beau did.

"I just saw my daughter having lunch with a friend. She didn't seem happy. There's no problem with you and my daughter, is there?" he asked, his tone making it clear that if there was, then it was Oliver's fault.

"No. Why would you think it had something to do with me?" Oliver had the bad feeling that his father-in-law knew more about Rebecca's state of mind than her own husband did. Had Rebecca said something to her father? Had she told him about the conversation she'd overhead last night on the phone?

He felt himself begin to sweat as Beau didn't answer the question—instead just studied him thoughtfully before taking a sip of his coffee.

"You said Dixie has taken off?" Anything to get the conversation off him and Rebecca. Even talking about his *least* favorite subject, Dixie.

Beau sighed and took a sip of his coffee. Oliver tried to remember the last time he'd seen his father-in-law drink coffee instead of Scotch this time of the day and couldn't.

"Did Dixie say anything to you?" Beau asked, settling his gaze on Oliver.

"No," he said, unable to hide his surprise. He spoke with Dixie even less than he did with his own wife. "Why would she tell *me* anything?"

"You *are* her brother-in-law, or don't you see her, either?"

Oliver didn't like the edge to Beau's voice. He plunged in, figuring it might be easier if they just got it out of the way right now. "Is there something I've done to upset you, Beau?"

The older man seemed to give that some thought. "I'm just worried about my daughters." His expression didn't change though. Oliver told himself he'd better watch his step. Something more had set Beau off and since he and Beau had never been close and now Chance Walker was in the picture…

He tried to assure himself this was just about Dixie. Beau's youngest had kept him upset more often than not over the years. What had she done this time? Oliver wondered.

"I've hired someone to find Dixie," Beau was saying. "Once she's back in Texas…" Beau rose awkwardly from the chair and Oliver realized with satisfaction that the oilman was getting old. Beau looked embarrassed to be seen at all feeble in front of him. "If you hear from Dixie…" He seemed to realize how unlikely that would be.

Like Oliver, he must have been wondering why he'd come in here to begin with. Or maybe he'd just been testing him, waiting for his son-in-law to hang himself. But then, Oliver had been feeling more than a little paranoid lately.

"I'll let you know if I hear anything," Oliver lied.

Right now, his only thought was Rebecca. Had she gone to her father about him? Her timing couldn't be any worse with him under so much strain. This deal had to go through and in a hurry. His life depended on it.

In HIS REARVIEW mirror, Chance watched the tractor get smaller and smaller until they went around a bend and it disappeared. No sign of the SUV.

He looked over at Dixie, not surprised to see one arm around Beauregard's neck, the other hanging on to the door handle. Her face was still pale and for the first time, she looked scared.

"Is it my driving?" he joked.

She glanced over at him as if her mind had been a thousand miles away. "It's fine."

"Fine?" He snorted. "That was an amazing example of my driving ability and you say it was *fine?*"

He finally had her attention.

She smiled. She had a gorgeous smile. "I'd forgotten how full of yourself you are."

He smiled back at her, worried as hell. Based on the number of people after her, Dixie Bonner was in a world of trouble.

The problem was that while she'd said she'd come all the way to Montana because he was the only person she could trust, she no longer trusted him. So getting her to tell him what was going on could pose a problem.

Well, all that was about to change, Chance told himself as he saw a sign for a mountain lodge just ahead. He didn't slow down until he reached the turnoff and pulled off onto the snow-packed gravel road.

Still no sign of the SUV.

But he had a bad feeling it wasn't the last they'd see of the people after Dixie Bonner.

And soon he would know why.

Dixie glanced back, more relieved than Chance could know that he'd lost the SUV. She watched him shift the pickup into four-wheel drive as he headed up the snowy road, wondering where he was taking her.

It hadn't slipped her mind that Chance was working for her father. Who knew what kind of deal they'd made?

Just the thought made her sick to her stomach. She'd thought Chance was the one person who couldn't be bought by her father. If she'd been wrong about Chance, then what hope was there?

"Where are we going?" she asked, worried. Ahead, all she could see was a mountain, the road disappearing into the snowcapped pines and what appeared to be a wide expanse of roofline.

"Somewhere safe," was all he said as he drove up the winding road, but she could feel his gaze on her every few minutes, as if he had a lot of questions.

She was sure he did.

She had a lot herself. She'd been so sure that once she had found him, all she had to do was to pour her heart out to him and he would be there for her.

Now she wasn't sure what to do next. Trusting Chance could be her worse—and last—mistake. So far he hadn't believed anything she'd told him.

She hated to even think what he would say when she told him the rest.

"I'm going to help you," he said quietly, as if sensing her wrestling with the problem.

She could only nod. Whatever he had planned for her, she would figure out a way to keep one step ahead of him. Hadn't she gotten this far all by herself? She didn't kid herself that a lot of it had been luck. Her would-be killers hadn't expected her to go to Montana.

No, she decided. Trusting Chance now would be a mistake. Better to keep her options open and try to get away from him the first opportunity that presented itself.

"Montana is so beautiful," she said, trying to hide the affect her decision had on her. She turned to look out the side window, secretly brushing away her tears. She'd been such a fool. All these years of comparing every man she met with Chance. He had been her hero. The man of her dreams.

"Well, you've apparently seen a lot of the state, I'll give you that," Chance said.

She turned to look at him, almost as angry with him as she was disappointed in him. "I wondered why you stayed here. I guess you weren't just hiding out from my father and Rebecca."

"I'm not the one who has the whole state of Texas after her."

She ignored that and saw him check his rearview mirror. "Did my father tell you about his heart attack?"

"Is this just chitchat or are you leading up to something?" he asked, cutting his eyes to her. "Like maybe the truth about what's really going on."

The truth? She had to smile. Even if he hadn't been hired by her father, there was another reason she was reluctant to tell him. There wasn't a chance in hell that he was going to believe her.

"I just thought you'd want to know the score. The doctor said the heart attack was minor but that he had to slow down," she continued. "Unfortunately he's too controlling to turn over the reins, not even to Mason. Forget Uncle Carl, he wants nothing to do with running an empire, and Ace would steal every dime. I think Daddy isn't so naive he doesn't know that. Nor would he ever give Oliver control. Oliver is Rebecca's husband." She glanced over at him. "Daddy can't stand him. Uncle Carl says if Daddy keeps giving Oliver enough rope, he'll hang himself and Rebecca will be the best-dressed widow at the funeral."

"I see you're still getting along well with your family," he said.

"You have no idea."

Chance could feel her gaze on him but he kept his eyes on the road and his mouth shut. She was just trying to get a rise out of him. And damned if it wasn't working.

"I guess *Daddy* didn't tell you that he's also getting into politics?" she said.

He noticed the contemptuous way she said "Daddy." He wondered if she was making fun of her father and her relationship with him. Or if this was about Rebecca since, as he recalled now, she'd always called Beau "Daddy."

Either way, it made him all the more convinced that this drama was just some power struggle between Dixie and her *daddy*. And it made him mad as hell that he'd gotten involved. Especially for *money*.

"Beauregard and I didn't do a lot of talking," Chance

said after a few moments, curious, though, where she was headed with all this. She'd seemed vulnerable a few moments ago and he'd made the mistake of being nice to her. She didn't react well to sympathy.

"I'm not surprised he's going into politics, though," Chance admitted. Money and politics seemed to go together and Beauregard Bonner had his fingers in anything that would benefit him. Given his money and his need for power, it had been just a matter of time before he got into politics. "But if your father is so powerful in Texas, then why didn't you let him help you out of whatever mess you're in?"

"You wouldn't believe me if I told you," Dixie said, looking away. "After all, you still don't believe that someone is trying to kill me."

"Now why wouldn't I believe you? Let's see. One, you haven't given me one reason why anyone would want you dead. Two, you don't seem to have been kidnapped, but someone is trying to get a million and a half out of your rich old man—and they just happened to have your locket. Three, your father doesn't want to go to the feds or the police any more than you do. Four, he's hired not one, but a bunch of guys just to haul you back to Texas as if he has some reason to believe it might be difficult and a necessity. Five, you seem pretty damn relaxed for someone who supposedly has killers after her."

"You have no idea how scared I am," she snapped. "Would it make you feel better if I were hysterical, crying and wringing my hands and begging you to tell me what to do?"

For a few moments there was only the crunch of the

tires on the cold snow, the dog's soft snores and the steady throb of the pickup's engine.

Chance kept his mouth shut, knowing that anything he said would be wrong.

"Look," Dixie finally said. "I've been taking care of myself for quite a few years now. Because of who my father is, I've always had to be careful. Most of the men I meet just want my father's money. Even some women try to befriend me for the same reason. From the time I could walk I was told I had to watch out for kidnappers." She cocked her head at him. "Is it any wonder I kidnapped myself to get what I wanted a few times when I was younger?"

He said nothing, unable to imagine her life. He'd come from middle-class parents, an adequate house but no pool. As a kid, he'd gotten a paper route to make extra money, then lawn-mowing jobs later. After high school, to help save for college, he'd gone to work in one of Beauregard Bonner's oil fields for the summer. That was until he'd inadvertently caught the attention of Bonner himself, who'd hired him as security for his daughters even though Chance was only a few years older than Rebecca.

Bonner had liked him, noticed how hard he worked in the field, and come up with the job. Maybe Bonner had hoped all along that Chance would marry his oldest daughter. Or maybe that was the last thing he'd ever wanted.

"I told you why I was waiting for you at the museum."

"Right. You were just making my life easier along with making it easier for the guys in the black car."

"You really have become incredibly cynical and not very trusting."

He laughed. "You're a *Bonner*. And I haven't forgotten what you were like as a kid."

"Those were just childish pranks," she said with a wave of her hand.

"Like kidnapping yourself."

She looked away. "I'll admit I've made a few mistakes in the past. But whether you believe it or not, I've changed."

He nodded, not believing it. "Your father doesn't believe you've changed."

She glared over at him. "Since when have you started trusting my father? I thought you were smart enough that you would remember my father *always* has ulterior motives for everything he does."

"He says he's trying to protect you."

She laughed. "And you believe that?"

He thought about Jamison, the duct tape in the back of the van.

"I can't go back to Texas or they'll kill me."

"You already said that. But what I'd like to know is why you didn't just come straight to my office instead of zigzagging your way across Montana."

She gave him a how-ignorant-are-you look. "That would have been pretty stupid, don't you think? Obviously someone knew where I was headed. My father, for instance. And how do you suppose someone knew to break into your office and steal the answering machine tape with my messages?"

He wished he knew.

"What is wrong with you?" she demanded angrily. "Don't you see? My father *had* to get to you first. He had to make you distrust me. I'm sure he offered you some outrageous amount of money. He knew I'd come to you. He had to make sure you wouldn't believe me when I told you why they want me dead. And he had to make sure you didn't get my messages."

"Are you trying to tell me your father is in on this? He's the one who gave me the record of your credit card charges. Why would he do that if he didn't want me to find you?"

"He wanted to make sure you didn't believe anything I told you," she said with a quirk of her brow. "Worked, didn't it?"

Chance wanted to argue the point but knew she was right at least about his preconceived notions about her—and where he'd gotten most of them.

He watched her rub one of Beauregard's big ears. The dog moaned softly and snuggled against her.

Don't get used to that, Beauregard. Dixie Bonner is on her way back to Texas just as soon as I can get her butt on a plane.

Chapter Seven

Dixie looked up as Chance slowed the pickup. A building appeared from out of the snowy pines draped in red and green lights. Hot Springs Lodge. The log structure was set against a backdrop of rocky cliffs and snowcapped trees. It was as picturesque as anything she'd ever seen, even with the Santa Claus and sleigh with the silhouettes of reindeers out front.

"Is that where we're going?" After Chance moved to Montana, she'd read everything she could get her hands on about the state. This is exactly how she'd pictured a Montana mountain lodge.

She tensed as she heard a buzzing sound off to her right and looked in her side mirror to see a snowmobile racing along beside the pickup just a few yards off the road. Behind it was a half dozen more snowmobiles.

Chance parked in front of what appeared to be a full-fledged Montana resort complete with log hotel, storefront café, gift shop and hot springs.

"You approve?" he asked, sounding amused.

"I love it. They have food and a *pool*."

He chuckled. "I forgot how much you liked to eat— and swim—as a kid. I guess some things don't change."

She met his gaze. He was smiling at her, the look in his eyes so familiar. Who knew what Chance had promised her father when Beauregard had hired him? But at that moment, Dixie weakened. She would have bet everything that she hadn't been wrong about Chance Walker, that he was still her hero, that ultimately he would save her.

She told herself it had nothing to do with the fact that he looked so darned good. Or that she'd missed him. She'd once thought that Chance would always be around. She'd been more devastated than Rebecca when Chance hadn't come back to Texas.

But was she willing to stake her life on him?

The driver of the lead snowmobile stopped in front of the lodge.

"I'll be right back," Chance said, apparently recognizing the man. "I'll get us a couple of rooms, some food and then we're going to have a talk."

Her stomach somersaulted. "Great. But what's the point if you aren't going to believe me?"

"You're going to *convince* me," he said with a grin, and opened his pickup door.

She watched him go over to the large man still straddling the snowmobile, the motor rumbling, the exhaust puffing out gray clouds into the cold late afternoon.

The other riders took off in a beehive of noise and activity. Dixie couldn't hear what was being said, but she saw Chance tell the man on the snowmobile something that made him glance in her direction. Then the man started up the snowmobile again and followed after the others.

Chance opened her side door. "We're all set."

She wondered what that meant. Dixie realized that neither of them had any luggage. She'd left what little she'd purchased in her car. She hadn't even thought to retrieve it, but then, she hadn't been thinking clearly for days now. And it wasn't as though Chance had given her much of an opportunity.

Her stomach growled.

Chance grinned, clearly hearing it.

She climbed out of the truck, the dog jumping out after her. Beauregard trotted along beside them as they entered the lodge, and Chance went behind the front desk to get a key.

Only one key?

Every daydream she'd ever had about Chance suddenly blossomed. She felt her face heat as her heart did a little Texas two-step. Around them Christmas music played softly. A white Christmas in Montana. It was more than she could have dreamed possible.

"There a problem?" he asked, cutting his eyes to her and grinning.

She really had to quit being so transparent.

"It's the family lodge unit," he explained. "*Two* bedrooms. One key. After all, someone is trying to kill you. I can't let that happen."

She made a face at him and looked around the lodge as she and the dog followed him up the stairs. The walls were log with a rich patina that had built up over the years. There was a huge stone fireplace, comfortable chairs and couches spread around it and a massive stuffed moose head on the wall. The moose was wearing a red and white Santa hat.

She couldn't believe she was in Montana, in a place like this and with Chance Walker. Too bad that's where the fantasy part ended.

"This way," Chance said.

She nodded and followed him down a rustic hallway, still looking around, taking it all in. Hadn't she imagined Chance Walker in just such a place? Only she'd always thought of him as the cowboy in the white hat who lived by the Code of the West. Which meant he would be on *her* side. Not her father's.

She'd truly believed he was the one person Beauregard Bonner couldn't manipulate. She realized now how naive that had been. Her father was the master manipulator. And what he couldn't manipulate he could afford to buy.

But then, she was pretty good at getting what she wanted, she reminded herself. After all, she'd learned from the best.

What would it take, though, to get Chance to believe her? she wondered as he unlocked their room and pushed open the door. The dog trotted in and Dixie followed.

The family lodge unit was spacious, much like a two-bedroom apartment. The walls were knotty pine and everything was decorated with prints of cute bears and even cuter moose.

She walked through the place, noting the only other exit was the second-floor deck. Something told her he'd picked this room because there would be little way for her to escape without him knowing it.

"I think I'll take a hot shower," she said, and smiled at him.

He glanced into the bathroom and smiled at her. There was no window. No way out. "I'll order us something to eat."

Once in the bathroom, she turned on the shower and let it run as she thought about her options. Try to get Chance to believe her? Or plan how she'd get away when he didn't?

THE MOMENT Beau left his office, Oliver called Rebecca's cell phone number. He had to know what she'd told her father without letting her know he'd seen her last night and that he knew she'd been eavesdropping on his phone conversations.

Her cell rang four times and just when he was starting to worry, she picked up.

"Dixie?" she asked, sounding out of breath. She hadn't had time to check the caller ID apparently.

"No, it's me." Why was she out of breath?

"Oh. Oliver." She sounded so disappointed he was instantly angry.

"Is everything all right?" he asked, masking his anger. "You sound out of breath."

"Fine."

"You were hoping it was Dixie," he said.

"Yes."

He gritted his teeth. Last night, after she'd overheard him on the phone, he'd gone up to their bedroom. He'd heard her breathing, had said her name. She hadn't answered and he couldn't see her in the dark. She kept their bedroom so damned dark he'd become adept at getting around it without stumbling over anything. And she often used earplugs even though the room was soundproofed. She didn't even want to hear him breathing at night.

He'd known she wasn't asleep—just pretending as usual. And that had been fine with him.

"I spoke with your dad," he said now and waited.

No response.

"I know Dixie's in Montana and that you're worried about her," he said.

"Is that what he told you?"

Had it always been this hard to talk to her?

"He told me he hired Chance Walker to find her."

Silence. She wasn't taking the bait.

"What are you doing for dinner?" He hated that he was forced to resort to a romantic dinner and probably making love to her.

"I have plans."

It had been months since they'd dined together. The nanny always fed the children early unless Beau was coming over. He had the feeling that they both avoided sitting across a table from each other and that's why they often had separate plans.

"It was just a thought," he said, relieved. At least he'd made the effort. He'd make sure Beau knew that he'd tried and it had been Rebecca who had *plans*.

"I might work late then," he said. "I have a ton of work to do."

Still nothing on her end. More than likely she knew it was a lie. Another reason he resented her.

Just like now. She was forcing him to fill the silence. "Have a nice evening then." He hung up, cutting off anything she might have said. Not wanting to know that all she'd done was hang up, as well.

He went to the bar and washed down antacids with alcohol, liking the way the alcohol burned all the way down. Damn the bitch. She was killing him.

WHILE DIXIE WAS IN the shower, Chance made the call to Bonner. "Dixie is with me," he said when the older man answered.

He heard relief and when Bonner spoke, he sounded choked up, making Chance feel guilty for questioning the oilman's motives. Maybe he really had just been worried about his daughter and believed he could keep her safe back in Texas.

That would explain why he was so insistent about getting her back there. Not to mention it was Christmas. Of course, he'd want her near him for the holidays. It wasn't as though Bonner had a reason he didn't want her in Montana.

"With the holiday, there won't be any flights out of here," Chance told him.

"I'll send my jet. Let me see when I can arrange it." Bonner put him on hold to check with his pilot.

The sooner the better, Chance thought, glancing toward the other room. He could hear the shower running, the bathroom door closed, and felt a strange stub of guilt. He'd purposely waited to call Bonner until Dixie was out of earshot.

Not that he hadn't been up-front about his plans. She

knew he was working for her father. He was just doing what he'd been paid to do.

So why did he feel like hell?

"The soonest, apparently, is the day after tomorrow about this time," Bonner said, coming back on the line. "You found her a lot quicker than I expected."

Chance swore under his breath. He'd hoped to be done with this assignment tomorrow. Forty-eight hours? Still, he should be finished with it and at his cabin by Christmas Eve.

"Okay, I'll bring her to the airport, but if she doesn't want to go with you, I won't help you force her," Chance said.

"Is Dixie *there?*"

"Yes. If you want to talk to her…"

Chance started to tell Bonner that she was in the shower in the adjacent room, but before he could, the old man said, "No. I'm just glad she's all right."

"Have you gotten any more calls from the kidnapper?" Chance asked, a little surprised Bonner wasn't asking the kinds of questions a father might ask when there was even a possibility that his daughter had been kidnapped.

"No. No more calls. Obviously, it was just a prank."

Chance frowned. "You think Dixie sent her locket to you?"

"Has she said anything?"

Anything? "Like what?"

"I don't know," Bonner said. "Dixie's always had a very active imagination. Who knows what story she'll make up to sway your opinion of her?"

"Well, she didn't imagine all the men you hired to bring her back to Texas."

Bonner either didn't hear what Chance said or ignored it. "Dixie can be very persuasive. Believe me, she'll try to con you in some way before this is over."

"Yeah? And what exactly is *this?*"

"Just a little family disagreement," Bonner said.

"Right."

"I'm just glad that Dixie is all right."

Whatever was going on, Dixie didn't seem all right. And Bonner seemed worried about what Dixie might tell him.

"By the way, have you gone over to her house?" Chance asked. "She says it was ransacked."

"Really? I can send someone over to check."

"Why don't you go yourself?" Chance suggested. "Maybe it will clear some things up."

"Things are clear enough," Bonner said. "Your job is to just make sure she's at the plane. There's a bonus in it for you if you get her there without any problems."

"I can't imagine why I'd have any problems, can you?" Chance asked facetiously.

"She's my daughter. That should tell you something." Bonner hung up before Chance could respond to that.

When he turned, he saw Dixie standing in the middle of the room. If looks could kill, he would have been dead as a doornail before he hit the floor.

"You called my father while I was in the shower," she said, her voice low and furious. But what cut him to the quick was her betrayed expression.

"It didn't really matter what I was going to tell you,

did it?" she said, advancing on him. "You'd already made up your mind that you were going to help ship me back to Texas one way or the other because that's what Daddy's paying you to do."

"Dixie, I wanted to let your father know you were all right."

She shook her head, smiling ruefully. "I heard you make arrangements for a jet."

"The plane isn't coming for forty-eight hours."

"How much is he paying you?" She raised a brow. "Knowing *Daddy,* he's even promised you a bonus, right?" She smiled as she must have seen the answer in his face. "How much?" she asked as she stepped to him, her body brushing against his in a way that told him what was coming next.

She smelled good. Her skin was flushed from her shower, her hair pulled up to expose her long slender neck. "Dixie—"

"I don't have as much money as my father, but now that we both know you can be bought, let's decide exactly what your price is," she said as she shoved him backward. He stumbled and dropped into one of the overstuffed chairs.

She bent over him.

"Don't." The word didn't come out with as much force as he'd hoped. "You don't want to do this."

She raised a brow. "You think this is worse than selling out to Beauregard Bonner?" She laughed and shook her head. "This is child's play compared to that."

"Dixie." A single lock of her hair brushed across his cheek as she bent closer, the movement emitting the sweet scent of her. Eyes locked with his, she brushed her lips over his. Just a promise of a kiss. It had been so long and his pain so deep, he'd thought no woman could ever arouse desire in him again.

He was wrong.

"Come on, Chance. What's it going to be?" she asked in a soft whisper near his ear, her warm breath caressing his neck.

It would have been so easy to let her seduce him. So easy. He grabbed her shoulders a little harder than he meant to and held her away as he pushed up from the chair, driving her back until they both stumbled into the living room wall.

He was breathing hard and one look in her eyes told him that she knew the effect she'd had on him. There was triumph in all that blue and yet he could feel her body trembling under his palms.

His gaze traveled over her face, lighting on her lips. How easy it would have been to kiss her. Not a light, teasing kiss like the one she'd just given him but a real honest-to-goodness kiss.

The thought shocked him because he wanted to kiss her senseless. He wanted to bury his fingers in her hair and to pull her to him until his body…

He let go of her, turning away, trying to hide the conflicted emotions that boiled up inside him. She wasn't just a job, she was Rebecca's little sister.

"I'm not my sister, Chance," she said, as if she knew what he was thinking, what he was feeling. "I *know* you," she said, stepping in front of him to block his escape.

He shook his head. "I'm not the man you think I am."

She cocked a brow at him. "You think putting me in a private jet and sending me back to Texas is any different from what the other men my father hired would do to me?"

"Dixie—"

"No, if that's what you want to do, then you're right. You aren't the man I knew. Or one I want to know."

"Your father believes that the only place you're going to be safe is Texas."

"Then you should listen to my father," she said, eyes blazing with anger before she spun around and headed out the deck door, slamming it behind her.

He swore as he watched her walk to the edge of the railing, her back to him. The light breeze stirred her hair. He could see her breath coming out in small white puffs. Forty-eight hours. Hadn't Bonner warned him not to let Dixie get to him? Just find her and take her to the plane. Period. Bonner had said it was a family matter. Let them work it out. It had nothing to do with him. Hell, what were the chances that anyone was really trying to kill her anyway?

He shook his head. He couldn't let himself get caught up in this little rich girl's fantasies. She was running a scam on her father. Upping the stakes to a million and a half. No wonder Bonner wanted Dixie stopped. He'd been through this with her before.

Not that any of that rationale helped the situation right now because Chance was caught in the middle, feeling guilty when it wasn't his fault that Dixie had purposely involved him by coming to Montana.

He groaned. Come to Montana because she'd said she thought he was the one person she could trust to help her.

He looked out on the deck. The sun had dipped behind the Big Belt Mountains. He swore and opened the deck door. Cold darkness had settled in the pines, the shadows growing long and black beneath them in the snow.

Quietly opening the deck door, he stepped out, joining her at the railing. He knew she had to be cold. She stood, her arms wrapped around her. As he looked over, he saw that her eyes were closed and she seemed to be breathing in the cold evening air as if gasping for breath. As he watched, two tears rolled down her cheek.

She seemed to sense him standing there. Her blue eyes came open. She turned away, brushed at the tears and took a moment before she looked at him.

He saw that she was embarrassed that he'd caught her with her defenses down. The men chasing her were enough to scare anyone. He leaned against the railing next to her and looked out at the snowy land. Ice crystals danced in the air like glitter.

"I should have told you I was going to call your father," he said quietly.

She made an angry sound. "Is it true you haven't married because you never got over Rebecca?"

His gaze flew to her. "Where did that come from?"

"Is it?"

"No." He looked back out at the valley. "I just haven't found anyone I wanted to marry. Do you always ask such personal questions?"

"Yes."

He realized she preferred seeing *him* off balance than the other way around. "What about you?"

"What *about* me?"

"Why aren't you married?"

"I'm too young." She grinned, her cocky attitude back.

"You're what? Thirty?"

"Twenty-nine and you know it." She shivered, wrapping her arms tighter around her. "It's cold out here." She started to turn to go back inside.

On impulse he grabbed her arm to stop her. "It's okay to be scared. It would help if I knew what you had to be afraid of, though."

She met his gaze and held it. "Yes, it would help, wouldn't it? But then you said you weren't interested. Your job was just to get me to that jet back to Texas." She pulled free and strode into the lodge, hips swinging, head high, the door slamming behind her.

Chance watched her go, cursing under his breath. Bonner had warned him that Dixie would play him. So what if she told him her side of the story? That didn't mean she'd tell him the truth.

But even as he thought it, he knew he'd let her get to him.

Chapter Eight

As Dixie heard Chance come in from the deck, there was a knock at the door. She'd told herself she wasn't hungry, but the smell of food made her stomach rumble as a young man from the lodge served what they called the Montana Special.

"Food," Chance said, as if offering an olive branch after the young man left.

She was still furious with him, but the food smelled too good and she caught sight of what looked like pie. She did love pie. And he knew it.

They consumed buffalo burgers, cattleman fries and moose-tracks chocolate milkshakes in silence.

"I thought you might like this," Chance said, handing her a piece of the pie. "It's huckleberry. A local favorite."

She took a bite. The food had taken the edge off her anger. That and the fact that Chance seemed to be trying to placate her.

"Bring your pie in here," he said, and got up to go into the living room area to sit in one of the plush recliners. His dog plopped down at Chance's feet to sleep off the two burgers he'd devoured. "So tell me what's going on, really," Chance said when she joined him.

She forked a bite of pie and ate it.

He leaned back, all his attention on her. "Dixie, talk to me. Why is someone trying to kill you?"

She told herself, why bother telling him? Even if he believed her, he was getting paid to take her to a jet in forty-eight hours because her father apparently was bound and determined to get her back to Texas—one way or another.

She looked into Chance's handsome face and feared she was about to make the biggest mistake of her life.

But at least it would be her last mistake.

CHANCE WAITED, remembering how stubborn she'd been as a kid. She hadn't changed that much, he realized. She was furious with him. Not that he could blame her.

"Let me make it easy for you," he said. "Who was the guy chasing us on the highway?"

She bit at her lower lip for a moment. "Roy Bob Jackson. He works for my father."

"And? Come on, I know there's more to it. He seemed to want to talk to you about something."

She glanced away and sighed. "He probably just wants his engagement ring back."

Chance let out an oath. "He's your *fiancé?* And you didn't think to mention that while the guy was chasing us?"

"It's a long story."

"I bet it is," Chance said with a shake of his head. "So much so that you forgot to mention you were getting married."

"I'm not *marrying* the bastard."

"He gave you a ring!"

"No, he put it in my Christmas stocking."

Chance frowned. "You already looked in your stocking?"

Dixie mugged a face at him. "You know I could never wait until Christmas Day."

He'd forgotten how she was always snooping around the tree, shaking packages. "So the guy left a ring and a note asking you to marry him? Romantic."

"He couldn't look me in the eye and do it."

"So you never told him your answer?"

"My life got a little complicated right after that."

He shook his head in disbelief. "Now you won't even *talk* to him?"

"He works for my father. He lied to me. I'm sure *Daddy* set him on me, deciding I needed a husband," she said, looking away as if embarrassed that she'd been played the fool.

Bonner just never learned. Is this what was going on between father and daughter?

"Where is the engagement ring now?"

"In my purse."

He raised a brow. "You just happen to have it? You must have been at least thinking about accepting it."

"I'd planned to throw it in his face."

"If you'd have told me, I could have stopped the pickup."

"For all I know my father sent Roy Bob to try to convince me to forget all this."

"This?" Chance said. "The two men who jumped you in the parking garage?"

She nodded. "I was at the library doing research."

"Research? You mean, like for a *job?*"

She sighed. "You know it really ticks me off that you think I'm just a younger version of my sister. I work for a newspaper."

"I didn't know Beauregard owned a paper." He quickly laughed and held up his hands. "Just joking."

She looked over at him with murder in her eye. "It so happens that I majored in journalism and I'm one hell of an investigative reporter. I've won awards, damn you."

Her outburst seemed to amuse him.

"You just assume that I couldn't get a job unless my father got it for me?"

"I'm sorry, okay? Tell me about your research. Was it for something you were working on at the paper? Maybe that's why you were attacked."

"No. It was personal research."

He raised a brow and she could already see the doubt in his eyes. She hesitated. But wasn't there the remote chance that she could convince him she was telling the truth? Otherwise, Chance Walker, her hero since she was twelve, would just be another man who'd let her down.

And she couldn't bear that.

Chance had tried to hide his surprise at hearing that Dixie had a real job. But from what Bonner had told him about his youngest daughter, who could blame him?

Why hadn't Bonner mentioned that Dixie was an investigative reporter? Obviously there was more to Dixie Bonner than he'd been led to believe. She'd been a mouthy, tough kid. Now she was a woman with one hell of a fiery temper and a lot more grit than he would have expected given the family money and social status.

"I recently found out that I had family I knew nothing about," she said.

He nodded. "And?"

"And it's going to get me killed unless I can convince you to help me."

He shook his head to clear it. "Wait a minute." He scratched his head. He'd been hoping it would be the kind of investigative reporting that would explain her story about the abduction in the parking garage. "Okay, let me get this straight. This has something to do with *genealogy?*"

"I should have known you wouldn't understand," she snapped, and got up to go to the window.

"I'm sorry. I'm *trying* to understand."

She turned from the window. "The men who attacked me were after my research and the photographs."

"Photographs?"

"They're what started it," Dixie said with an impatient sigh. "I found three old photographs in a jewelry box that Uncle Carl gave me when I turned sixteen. He said he found it, but I knew it had belonged to my mother from the way my father reacted when he saw it." She sounded close to tears. "It's the only thing I had of my mother's."

Chance held his breath as Dixie went to her purse, opened it and took out a small envelope. From it, she withdrew three black-and-white snapshots.

"The men who abducted you didn't get the photographs?" He couldn't help sounding skeptical.

"They left my purse in the car when they went into

the house for the rest of my research materials," she said and, with obvious reluctance, held out the photographs to him.

He took them, treating them as she had, as if they might disintegrate.

"The photographs were hidden beneath the velvet liner of the jewelry box. I would never have found them if I hadn't bumped against the box and seen a corner of a photo sticking out."

He felt the hair rise on the back of his neck as he looked down at the first photograph. It was of a woman and a baby. He turned it over. On the back in a small delicate script were the words "Glendora and nephew Junior."

He set the photo on the coffee table. The next was of the woman Glendora and another older woman who resembled her. Both were standing at graveside. It was raining, the day dark. Both women wore black veils, their faces in shadow, but he recognized the Glendora woman by her shape. He turned the photo over. "Junior's funeral."

The third photograph was of a baby being held by the woman identified as Glendora. On the back, it read "Rebecca and Aunt Glendora."

He felt his heart do a little dip and flipped the snapshot back over to stare down at the baby, then at Dixie.

She nodded. "It seems Rebecca and I have an Aunt Glendora."

"You showed these to your father?" he guessed.

She nodded. "He said the jewelry box wasn't my mother's, he'd never seen the people in the photographs before and that it was just a coincidence that the baby's name was Rebecca."

"Quite the coincidence," Chance agreed.

Dixie took a breath and let it out slowly. "My father swears there never was a Beauregard Junior. Nor did my mother have a sister."

"Maybe that's the case."

Dixie shook her head. "I believed that, too, until he insisted on getting rid of the photographs for me. When I refused to give them to him, he became upset. I knew then that he was lying."

Or at least had something to hide, Chance thought as he looked at the snapshots again, then at Dixie. "So that's when you decided to dig into your family history."

She nodded. "You know me so well."

Didn't he, though. He'd thought this woman would be a stranger to him, that she would have changed so much he wouldn't know her. He'd been wrong about that. He wondered what else he might be wrong about.

"So you've been trying to find evidence of the people in the photographs."

She nodded and sat across from him.

"And you believe the two men who attacked you were after your genealogy research," he said carefully, trying not to make her mad again but hoping to point out how foolish that sounded.

"When the men were ransacking my house, they were looking for my research materials—and my journal."

He recalled that she'd always kept a journal from the time she was little. Rebecca had teased her about it.

It's a journal about my life—not a diary about which boy said I was cute, Dixie snapped.

Oh, please, Rebecca said. What does a twelve-year-old have to write about?

"Did they find your journal?" he asked.

"I would assume so. I always kept the original photographs with me in my purse. But I also made copies."

Smart woman. "Did your journal have information about this in it?"

She nodded, her gaze almost pleading for him to believe her. "Nearly everything I'd found out was in the journal."

"*Nearly* everything?" he repeated.

She didn't seem to hear him. "How much do you know about my mother, Sarah Worth Bonner?"

"Not much. She died when you were a baby."

"Thirteen months old. Rebecca was five. I think I remember Mother, but I'm not sure it isn't just something I made up, you know?"

He did. His parents had died when he was nineteen and he still wasn't sure a lot of the memories weren't ones he wished had happened.

"Over the years I've asked my father, but he always said he didn't like talking about her because it was too painful. For that reason supposedly, he kept no photographs of her."

Chance thought of his own daughter and the few cherished photographs he had of her. He wouldn't have parted with them for anything in this world.

"I started by trying to find out what I could about my mother through the usual sources, birth and death certificates, marriage licenses, social security," Dixie said, as if warming to her subject. "I found a marriage license and a death certificate, but no birth certificate. Social security had no record of her."

"Maybe she never worked," he suggested.

"Everyone has a social security card, but even if for some reason she didn't, she would definitely have had a birth certificate. That's not all. My father had told me my mother was an orphan with no siblings."

"You think this woman in the photograph is her sister."

Dixie nodded. "I know this doesn't seem like anything anyone but me would care about, except I found a record of a Glendora Worth. She would have been older than my mother. I remember Uncle Carl once telling me that my mother had been born up north. Glendora Worth was born in Ashton, Idaho."

He nodded. "Okay."

"There's more."

"I suspected there was."

"When the two men attacked me in the parking garage they were wearing masks, like I told you before. But when they came running out of the house and into the garage as I was getting away, they'd removed their masks and hadn't bothered to put them back on in their haste to stop me. I recognized one of the men. He works for my father."

Chance sat up abruptly. "You just mention this now?"

"You didn't believe that anyone was even trying to kill me. I knew what your reaction would be if I told you my father was behind it."

"Well, if you think I believe that your father paid two

hired guns to kill you so you wouldn't find out your mother had a sister—"

"See what I mean?" She let out a small bitter laugh and leaped to her feet. He grabbed her arm as she started past him, but she wrestled free and stalked over to the glass doors to the deck. "Don't you think it breaks my heart to think that my own father might be involved? But, Chance, I went to him when I found the photographs. I showed him what I'd found. He's the only person who knew."

He watched her place her forehead against the window, her breath condensing on the glass.

"Dixie, you have to admit, this sounds crazy," he said with a frustrated sigh. "It's just hard to believe that even if there was some deep, dark secret in your family, that *anyone* would have you killed to keep it quiet."

She didn't turn around, her voice was muffled. "You know how my father is. He does whatever he has to. I thought you would believe me since you know him. You know what he's capable of."

"Your father isn't responsible for breaking me and Rebecca up," he said.

"No," she said, turning from the window. "But he was responsible for getting you to Montana, wasn't he? You think that first job on the ranch just happened to open when you needed it? Or that scholarship to Montana State University?"

He stared at her. He'd always suspected Bonner was behind it. Things had worked out a little too well. "If you're insinuating that he got rid of me—"

"I'm telling you that he sold you down the river," she

said, stepping toward him, settling those big blue eyes on him. "Daddy was all for Rebecca marrying Oliver and we all know why."

"It doesn't matter. Rebecca and I would never have gotten married even if I'd stayed in Texas," he said, knowing in his heart it was true.

She nodded. "I agree. But it shows how low my father will stoop to get what he wants. He sold off Rebecca to further the Bonner name. You think he'd let anyone sully that name after everything he's done to get where he is today? Especially since he's about to throw his hat into the political ring."

Chance shook his head, not wanting to believe it. Hadn't Bonner warned him not to believe anything Dixie told him?

Dixie nodded and smiled as if sensing that even against his will he was starting to believe her. "I start digging into my family's background and now someone is trying to kill me. So, you still believe the two aren't connected and that my father isn't involved?"

Chapter Nine

"Hello, Mr. Lancaster."

Oliver was feeling better by the time he reached the club. He'd managed to put off thinking about the future. At least for tonight.

Rebecca had plans. What did it matter who they were with? He just needed to concentrate on the problem at hand—winning twenty-five thousand dollars.

"Your coat, Mr. Lancaster?"

He let the man help him out of his coat and get him a drink, thankful that men's clubs still existed, albeit underground. Otherwise some woman would protest and the next thing you knew, the place would be full of them and everything would be ruined.

"Any interesting games going on?" he asked as he took the drink. He didn't even have to tell the man what he drank. So much better than home where Rebecca was often out of his favorite.

No, he thought, looking around at the exquisite furnishings, this was his true home.

"I believe there is a game in the Ashbury Room that you might enjoy, sir."

Oliver smiled and asked for an advance, giving the man a hundred dollar bill before heading to the Ashbury Room.

He felt lucky tonight. At least he hoped so. If his luck didn't change soon, he would have no recourse but to do something desperate.

DIXIE COULD SEE that Chance was having the same trouble she was, trying to understand what she'd found—and why it had put her life in jeopardy.

"Before you tell me I'm crazy, you should know. Glendora Worth is still alive. From what I've been able to find out, her name is Glendora Ferris now." Dixie hesitated, bracing herself for his reaction to the rest of the news. "She's widowed and living in an apartment for elderly people in Livingston."

"Montana?"

She nodded. "Don't give me that look. I came to Montana to hire you just like I said. It's not my fault Glendora Worth Ferris just happens to live here."

"So what did she say when you saw her?"

Dixie shook her head. "I haven't yet. I wanted you to go with me. To keep me safe." She glanced at him. "Okay, I didn't want to go alone. Are you happy?"

He smiled. "You were smart to wait. If you're right…" He stopped as if catching himself. "I'm not saying I'm buying any of this—especially the part about your father trying to have you killed, okay? And you can't be certain this Glendora Worth is your mother's sister, right?"

"No. But what if she is?"

"Then you would have an aunt you knew nothing

about," he said. "But it wouldn't give anyone a motive to want you dead. This isn't much of a secret, Dix. So you have an aunt."

"And a brother who died."

"Did you find any record of a Beauregard Bonner Junior?"

"No," she had to admit.

Chance raised a brow as if that proved something.

"That's why I have to see this woman. If she really is my aunt, maybe she can provide the answers I need."

His gaze locked with hers. "What if your father is trying to protect you?"

"By having me killed?"

"I'm serious, Dixie. Maybe there's a reason he doesn't want you to know about this." He waved a hand through the air. "Maybe it's painful. Or dangerous."

She laughed. "Apparently it is. You still don't believe I was abducted in Texas, do you? You think I made it all up? Why would I do that?"

"To involve me in this."

Her heart was beating too hard, her pulse loud in her ears. "I can't believe you. I knew my father would try to find a way to stop me from getting to Glendora. I just never dreamed it would be you." She picked up the photographs and put them back in her purse. "I think I'll turn in early. I haven't had much sleep the last few days."

"Dixie."

She started toward her room, but turned to look back at him. "By the way, you didn't use the lodge phone to call my father, did you?"

He looked surprised.

"Because if you did, then he knows where we are." She nodded. "You just signed my death warrant."

CARL BONNER STOOD behind the two-way mirror that allowed him to look into the Ashbury Room and watch the poker game—and Oliver Lancaster.

Carl had kept an eye on Oliver from the first. Not that he'd told Beau. He watched Oliver dig himself a hole the arrogant bastard would never be able to climb out of.

"How much has he lost?" Carl asked the man who'd let him into this room.

"Tonight? Over a hundred thousand."

Carl said nothing as he mentally totaled just how deep Oliver was down. And the fool kept playing, like all gamblers, believing eventually he would win.

He'd never liked Oliver and over the years had grown to despise him. Oliver was a lousy husband and father. Carl was tired of seeing the man hurt Rebecca.

Carl watched Oliver sweat. Beauregard paid Oliver well, but not well enough to lose this kind of money almost every night of the week. Oliver had to be getting desperate to cover his compulsive gambling—and his debts. He couldn't go to Beauregard. Nor Rebecca.

So who did that leave poor Oliver?

Ace, Carl thought, with a smile. Only Oliver would be stupid enough to go to a known criminal for help.

"Put more pressure on him," Carl told the man waiting next to him. "Let him play, though. Don't worry, I'll see that he meets his obligations."

"As you say, sir."

Yes, Carl thought as he left. As I say. Carl turned and saw another window, this one into the Bradbury Room. Like other nights he'd come here to check on Oliver, Carl saw Mason sitting at one of the poker tables.

"What about Mr. Roberts?" Carl asked.

The man hesitated and Carl had to look hard at him for a moment before the man said, "He enjoys a good game. He wins some, loses some. He always quits before he loses too much."

Yes, that sounded just like Mason. Careful. But still a gambler at heart.

"You can tell a lot about a man by the way he plays cards, don't you think?" Carl said.

"Yes, sir. I assume that's why you don't play."

Carl laughed. Life was enough of a gamble, he thought as he followed the man out. Not that a man didn't have to take chances. Otherwise, he was doomed to live a truly mediocre existence. No one knew that better than Carl Bonner. He remembered the day that he'd changed his luck and his life so many years before—with just one roll of the dice.

CHANCE STARED AT Dixie's closed bedroom door and told himself that she was just being dramatic. While the family photographs were intriguing, he still didn't believe Bonner was behind any threat to his daughter over some old snapshots.

So why couldn't he quit mentally kicking himself for calling Bonner on the lodge phone? Beauregard Bonner was a lot of things. But a killer?

Chance swore, the cold December night pressing

against the windows as he saw a few lights glitter in the distance.

Hell, he was a professional and right now he felt like a damned amateur. What if Dixie was right and he'd put her life in jeopardy?

Worse, he was starting to believe her.

What bothered him was how easily he'd bought into what Bonner had told him about Dixie. That and the fact that she *was* his daughter. That's why Chance had given Dixie the room with a window, but no way out other than the door she'd just closed.

"Hell, what if she's right?" he asked himself again as he checked to make sure the doors were locked before going to his room. He left the bedroom door open. It was that darned suspicious nature of his.

It was going to be a long night. He hadn't gotten that much sleep last night after seeing Bonner and taking this job against his better judgment. He would have loved nothing better than a hot shower, but he opted for a bath, leaving the bathroom door open so he could hear Dixie if she tried to leave.

The hot water felt good. He tried to relax. Less than forty-eight hours and Bonner would send a jet for his daughter.

Chance had always prided himself on the fact that he could read people pretty well. But he had to admit there was too much water under the bridge to do that with Beauregard Bonner. Because he didn't trust him, he tended to go the other way and cut him more slack than he probably should have.

As for Dixie... Just the thought of her stirred

emotions he didn't want to acknowledge, let alone deal with. He remembered earlier, her leaning over him, that light kiss on his mouth—

Standing up in the bath water, he turned the water to cold and stood under it. Although painful, the cold shower did the trick. He turned it off and got out.

Toweling dry he smiled at his own foolishness. The woman knew the affect she had on him. Had on a lot of men. Like her almost-fiancé, who had also followed her to Montana.

Or been sent by Beauregard Bonner?

Chance hated to think how Bonner had set him up all those years ago. The job in Montana. The scholarship. It was hard to be angry. Chance was thankful for the life he enjoyed now. But it did remind him how Bonner operated.

He pulled on his jeans and sprawled on the bed. He knew he wasn't going to be able to sleep now even if he wanted to. He couldn't get Dixie off his mind. Wasn't there a song like that in Texas?

He got up, too restless to even lie on the bed. Keeping his eye on Dixie's closed bedroom door, he pulled on his coat and went out on the deck. He made a couple of calls, using his usual sources to get confidential information that the average person couldn't access.

There was a Glendora Ferris living in Livingston, just as Dixie had said. A couple more inquiries and he had her maiden name: Worth. The same as Dixie's mother's maiden name. The same information Dixie had gotten.

Was it possible Glendora really was Sarah's sister? More to the point, was there some deep, dark family secret that Dixie had stumbled across that someone was determined she would take to her grave?

He swore again as he stepped back in from the cold, closed the deck door and walked over to tap on Dixie's bedroom door. He figured she wouldn't be asleep yet.

"Yes?"

"If you want, we could go to Livingston first thing in the morning and talk to Glendora Ferris." He didn't have to add that the woman could have moved, might be senile, might not even be the right Worth. Nor did he have to tell Dixie that he wasn't anxious to get involved any further in this.

He heard a surprised sound on the other side of the door, could almost hear her smile. He started to step away from the door.

"Chance?"

"Yeah?" he said, moving back to the door again.

"Thank you."

He touched the door with the tips of his fingers. "Yeah."

NOT LONG AFTER midnight, Chance heard the lodge room door open and close quietly. He glanced at the clock, gave her a few seconds, then picked up his gun.

He had stayed dressed in his jeans expecting something like this. And yet, he couldn't help being surprised. And disappointed. He'd started to buy into her story. He'd even agreed to take her to talk to Glendora Ferris. So had it all been just a ruse?

He pulled on his coat and boots. Opening the door quietly, he peered out. Dixie tiptoed down the hallway dressed in jeans and a T-shirt, no shoes.

He frowned. No shoes? Where was she going bare-foot in December in Montana?

She had something tucked under her arm.

He waited until she turned the corner before he went after her. At the L in the hallway, he stopped to peer around the corner. She stood at the door to the hot springs outdoor pool. Even from where he was he could see that the pool was clearly marked closed for the night.

He watched her with interest since he suspected the door to the pool was kept locked at night.

She pulled the barrette from her hair she'd used to tie it back earlier. It took her a few minutes but to his amazement, she picked the lock and slipped in.

She was going *swimming?*

He hurried down the hallway only to find the door locked again. He'd never been great at lock picking, but he was hell on wheels when it came to fence climbing. Backtracking he circled around the rear of the lodge to come out at the fence along the dark side of the pool.

Steam rose off the surface, dissipating into the cold darkness. For a moment he didn't see her and thought she'd given him the slip. But then he spotted her discarded clothing piled on one of the chairs near the deep end, a towel lying on top.

At the sound of a splash, he saw her surface halfway down the pool in a cloud of steam and was surprised how relieved he was. She hadn't tried to get away. She'd just wanted to go for a swim. He smiled, shaking his head. Would this woman ever quit surprising him?

She dove back under the water and he quickly

climbed the wooden fence, moving to the edge of the pool as she surfaced.

He remembered that she'd been part fish back in Texas, always in her family pool. Always calling, "Hey, Chance, watch this." Even back then she'd loved attention. And had known no fear, diving off the highest thing she could find if it would shock him. He realized she hadn't changed.

He'd expected to surprise her, but if he did, she hid it well.

"Hello, Chance," she said with a grin.

"The pool is closed, Dixie. Also, I believe swimsuits are required."

Her grin broadened. "Why would anyone swim in a suit if she didn't have to? And close a pool on a night like this?" She looked up, her face softening. "Look at those stars. I had no idea there were so many." Her breath came out on a puff of frosty December air.

He saw that her hair was starting to freeze. Frost glistened on her eyelashes. A snow angel. Her beauty took his breath away.

She must have seen his expression because her gaze heated as it met his. Her smile widened. Oh, that mouth. Incredible full lips that arched up in a perfect bow that any man would have been a fool not to want to kiss.

She laughed and ducked under the water, disappearing beneath the steam—but not before he'd glimpsed her sleek naked body moving through the water.

Chance swore and glanced toward the lodge and the rooms that faced in this direction. Several of the blinds were open, lights out, but he'd bet Dixie had an audience and unless he missed his guess, she knew it and was enjoying it. "Damn it, Dixie."

As she surfaced, her laugh filled the air. "You should see your expression."

"You like shocking people."

She turned serious. "You're wrong. I just like swimming naked on a night like this."

Clouds scudded across the stars and with a suddenness that pretty much summed up Montana weather, it began to snow. The flakes were huge and, like delicate white feathers, drifted lazily down. Dixie laughed, the delight of a child, and leaned back to catch one in her mouth.

"You don't know what you're missing," she said, looking at him again through the steam rising up off the surface of the pool. He got the feeling she wasn't talking about swimming.

She cocked her head at him. "Sure you don't want to join me?"

"Positive." His voice sounded odd to him and he knew she'd heard it.

"I won't look if you're shy." She chuckled then turned her back, daring him to strip and join her.

He'd been tempted plenty times in his life, but this one topped the list.

"Scared?" she asked in that Texas drawl of hers.

"Aren't you worried your killers will find you? You are rather…exposed."

She turned back to give him a disappointed look. "You aren't going to spoil this for me, Chance Walker."

Her words hit him like stones. He hated that he'd even tried. But damn it, his job was to keep her safe. And he hadn't wanted this job. He should have been at his cabin with his dog and a roaring fire, not standing out here in the cold watching the damned woman swim naked in a closed pool.

Hell, if there had been a sign that said, No Diving, she would have been doing a jackknife off the side right now.

He reminded himself who she was. Not just a Bonner, which was bad enough, but Rebecca's little sister. Unfortunately that didn't help. Rebecca had been a lifetime ago.

He turned his back and listened to her swim, fighting the ache inside him. There'd been something about Dixie Bonner at twelve that had been likeable even though a lot of the time she was an impossible noisy little brat.

But the grown-up version was everything that had made Dixie unique at twelve—and a whole hell of a lot more.

After a while, he heard her climb out, listened to her pull on the jeans and T-shirt.

"You can turn around now."

He did.

She stood, her head cocked to one side, looking at him through a wet wall of dark hair. She brushed her hair back from her face and grinned, no doubt at his expression. She'd dried with the towel she'd carried under her arm from the room, and had put her clothing on over her damp body. The T-shirt clung to her breasts, leaving little to his imagination. There was no way she wasn't aware of that, as well.

"Your hair is starting to freeze," he said, mad at himself, mad at her. It was all he could do to keep from tossing her into the pool, clothes and all—and jumping in after her.

And that, he realized, is what really had him upset. He wished now that he'd gone in the pool with her, for he feared that when he was a very old man this would be his one regret in life.

"Let's get you back to the room," he said, taking off his jacket to put it around her.

She let out an amused laugh. "I never knew you were such a prude. You should have come into the pool," she said as she wrapped her long hair in the towel, her back to him. "You have no idea what you missed."

He cursed softly, just imagining.

She turned to grin at him. "You know I'm starting to understand why my sister didn't marry you."

"I was the one who broke it off with her," he snapped, instantly regretting it.

Her brow shot up. "Very gallant of you to admit that."

He swore under his breath. "I didn't mean it to come out like that. Hell, why am I apologizing? Your sister was already practically engaged to some blue-blooded lawyer student by then."

"You could have come back to Texas and put up a fight for her," she said over her shoulder as she walked toward the door to the lodge.

"Oh, yeah, that would have done a lot of good."

She grinned back at him. "You should have heard what she said about you. She said—"

"Don't even." He thought about some of the things Rebecca could have told her little sister and wished this subject had never come up.

Dixie laughed as they reached the door back into the lodge. Apparently it didn't lock from this side. "Didn't you ever wonder what your life would have been like if you'd stayed in Texas?"

"No," he lied. He stepped past her and into the lodge, planning to end this conversation by doing the only thing he could—run away from it.

"Did you know she kept a diary?" Dixie asked in a whisper as she caught up to him.

Rebecca kept a diary? He continued walking. The last thing he wanted to talk about was her sister. Especially after he'd just seen her little sister swim naked. Nor did it seem the right topic for a walk in the lodge hallway in the wee hours of the morning.

Dixie was probably bluffing anyway about the diary. But now that he thought about it, Rebecca was the type who would have kept a diary. One of those little pink ones with a lock and key. And Dixie was just the type to break into it and read it.

"Would you like me to quote you chapter and verse?" She didn't give him time to say no. "'Oh, today was just the most awful day,'" Dixie mimicked in a voice that was eerily like Rebecca's. "'Daddy forbade me to go out with that Chance Walker boy. My heart just ached and I cried throughout all of dinner but to no avail. Daddy was just impossible.'"

Chance groaned, the words sounding too much like Rebecca's for this not to be true. He stopped, turning to glare at her. "I'm surprised your sister didn't throttle you for reading her diary," he whispered back.

Dixie let out a snort. "She had no idea I ever read it. Rebecca, being Rebecca, wore the key around her neck and always kept the diary locked. Have you ever seen the flimsy locks on a diary?" Dixie chuckled. "I could pick locks a lot harder than that when I was seven."

All he could do was shake his head.

"Stop looking so shocked. I'm willing to bet you're no slouch when it comes to lock picking," she said as they reached their suite and she waited for him to open the door.

As he started to use the room key, he realized she'd expected him to follow her to the pool. That's why she hadn't even bothered to take the key. Or maybe she'd planned to pick the room lock, too.

"Only private detectives on TV pick locks," he snapped. "It's considered breaking and entering." He opened the door and, following her inside, closed it after them.

"Don't disillusion me with that legal mumbo jumbo. I've heard it all. Anyway, I wouldn't believe it." She grinned. "After reading Rebecca's diary, I know everything about you. And I do mean *everything*."

"Everything." He grumbled under his breath. "Just like your father." He saw the change in her expression.

"If you want to get along with me, don't compare me to him." She turned toward her room, her back stubborn-straight, her hips swaying from side to side in a way that could blind a man.

"Who says I want to get along with you?" he called after her. "You're the one who came to Montana. I didn't want this damned job to start with. I wanted nothing to do with your family."

"That's right," she called back over her shoulder. "I came to Montana. Looking for you. Because I had this crazy idea that you were one of the good guys. Instead, you go to work for my father. You didn't just sell out, Chance Walker. You broke my heart."

He saw her hesitate at her doorway as if she hadn't meant to add that last part. He wasn't sure why it touched him. He didn't even believe there were killers after her, right? Let alone that his going to work for her father had broken her heart.

"Do you still love her?"

He wasn't sure he'd known what love was until his daughter was born. "Rebecca? *No.*"

"Did *she* break your heart?"

"No." He hated to admit it. She'd been his first love. First loves were supposed to be ones you never got over, right?

"You were both so wrong for each other," Dixie said, shaking her head.

He couldn't argue that.

"You needed a woman who cared about more than what she was going to wear or whether her hair was just right or what her friends were going to say about her—and you."

He laughed since that was Rebecca to a T. She cared more about outward appearances than anything else. He hoped she was happy with…what was his name? Oliver?

"Like you know what kind of woman I needed," he said with a laugh, wanting to draw the subject away from Rebecca.

"Someone like…me," Dixie said, and disappeared into her bedroom, closing the door behind her.

He laughed, thinking she had to be joking.

In his room, he stripped down to his shorts and

sprawled again on the bed. He couldn't help but think about some of the things Dixie had said. He'd let her down and that bothered him more than he wanted to admit.

He tried to push her out of his mind, but the minute he closed his eyes all he could see was Dixie Bonner swimming through fog-cloaked water like a ghost mermaid, a million stars glittering overhead on a cold December night in Montana.

Chapter Ten

Chance bolted upright out of a deathlike sleep. He looked around, at first not sure where he was. As he came fully awake, he remembered it all—including the sound that had awakened him. The closing of a door.

Only he was pretty sure it was a neighboring door he'd heard from another unit.

Still, he jumped up and rushed into the living area. Dixie's door to her bedroom was standing open, her bed made. Had she even gone to bed last night?

In a panic, he checked her room, not sure what he thought he'd find. She'd had no luggage—just the clothing on her back, which he was pretty sure she'd taken with her. The room was empty. Dixie was gone.

Cursing, he stormed to the door and looked down the hallway. Empty. He glanced at his watch, then through a crack in the blinds on the deck doors. It was barely light out.

He felt foggy. He'd obviously drifted off at some point in the night, but didn't feel as if he'd gotten any rest. Who could blame him, knowing that Dixie Bonner was in the next room?

Or at least had been.

Where had she gone? He couldn't believe this. The woman was driving him crazy. Maybe that had been the plan all along.

Unless everything she'd told him had been a lie…

Or maybe she hadn't trusted him. Maybe she thought him no better than the others her father had hired to find her.

That thought grounded him like a crashed plane.

He rushed back into his room, threw on the rest of his clothing and hurried down to the lodge lobby, hoping she'd just gotten hungry and gone to breakfast.

"Have you seen the woman I had with me?" he asked the young man behind the desk who'd brought up their food. From the man's expression, he had. "Where did she go?"

"Said she wanted to take a walk." He pointed toward the window.

A walk? Chance turned to look out. The day was bright, the sky clear blue, the rising sun blinding on the snow, the temperature hovering around freezing. Was she crazy? Of course she was. She was a Bonner.

He could see a packed snowmobile trail that led out into the trees. "Is that the way she went?"

The young man nodded.

It hadn't been daylight long. She couldn't be that far ahead of him.

"It's an easy trail," the male clerk called after him as Chance ran for the door. "I'm sure she's fine."

Chance wished he could be sure of that. What had Dixie been thinking? Outside, he saw his friend who'd given them the suite for the night. "I need to borrow a snowmobile."

Two minutes later, Chance was roaring up the trail as it wound through the darkness of the trees, then rose up over a hill and into the faint morning sunlight. No sign of Dixie.

He should have caught up to her by now. What if the clerk was wrong? What if she'd taken another trail? Or what if she'd been right and his calling her father had the killers waiting outside—

He slowed and spotted her tracks in some soft snow that had fallen from a pine bough into the packed trail. She was running. From what?

Gunning the snowmobile, he raced up the trail as it curved and dipped in and out of the snowcapped pines. The cold winter morning air burned his face and lungs.

As he came around a curve in the trail, suddenly there she was. She'd heard the snowmobile coming and had stepped off the track.

"What's wrong?" he demanded as he shut off his machine and grabbed her, pulling her close as he drew his weapon. Hurriedly he searched the cold, dark shadows. The trees were dense here in the creek bottom, visibility poor.

"Nothing," she said, pulling free. "I just came out for a run."

He glanced over at her. "A *run?*"

"I like to run. It clears my head."

He stared at her as he slowly holstered his weapon and tried to still his thundering pulse. "Did you ever think that going for a run when there are so many people after you might be a bad idea?"

"No one knows we're here, right?"

Her reasoning was pushing him over the edge. "You're the one who said my call yesterday would have your father and his men breaking down our doors last night."

"I guess the lodge is harder to find than I thought," she shot back with a grin.

"What's so damned funny?"

"You. As you recently said to me, you can't have it both ways. Either you believe my life is in danger. Or you don't. Obviously, you do."

"You scared the hell out of me." It was out before he could call it back.

She cocked her head at him. "Admit it. You believe that someone wants me dead."

"Anyone who's ever met you probably wants to kill you," he said, his pulse finally dropping back to normal. Ice crystals glistened in the morning sunlight. The air smelled of pine and snow. And Dixie looked great.

"Whatever," she said with a little shake of her head just as she'd done when she was a kid and he'd wanted to turn her over his knee.

Some things just didn't change.

Beauregard Bonner had known where they were, but no hit men had shown up to take her out. That had to be one hell of a relief for her. She'd been wrong about her father.

"Ever been on a snowmobile?" he asked.

She shook her head, eyes wide and bright, her face suddenly alive with excitement.

He grinned. "Hop on."

The gunshot came out of nowhere. A tree just past Dixie's head splintered, the sound a loud crack that echoed across the mountainside. As he lunged for her, he heard the second shot. It whistled past his head as he tackled Dixie and took her down hard behind the snowmobile.

"You believe me now?" There were tears in her eyes. "I knew it. I knew it."

He cursed himself, his own stupidity. He shouldn't have made the call yesterday from the lodge phone. But he'd been so convinced that her father only had her best interests at heart. What the hell had he been thinking?

"Stay here and stay down," he ordered, pulling his weapon as he crouched behind the snowmobile, then made a run for it, dodging in and out of the trees, shielding himself as he moved quickly in the direction of the gunfire.

He could only estimate where the shot had come from, given where the first bullet had struck the tree. But as he moved, he came across the tracks in the fresh snow. They crisscrossed the mountainside, moving first in one direction, then back the other way.

Chance took off at a run following the tracks, keeping to the trees just as the shooter had. He hadn't gone far when he heard the sound of a vehicle engine turning over, then the spinning of tires in the snow.

It was hard to run fast enough through the snow. He reached the clearing just in time to see the sun catch on a rig's rooftop as it dropped over the side of the mountain. He couldn't tell what the vehicle had been, let alone the color with the sun glinting off it.

DIXIE WAS LYING in the snow on her back, staring up at the blue sky overhead. She didn't look in Chance's direction as she heard him approach, but she recognized the sound of his footfalls.

She'd been lying there, more frightened than she'd ever been before—even waking up in the trunk of her own car. Her fear had been not for herself but for Chance. She'd involved him in this and now she regretted it.

His shadow fell over her and she hurriedly wiped at her tears, not wanting him to see just how scared she was, how upset.

"I'm sorry," he said, and offered her a hand up.

She took it. "I'm the one who's sorry. I should never have gotten you into this," she said, brushing off what snow she could, her jeans caked with snow. But she didn't feel it. Felt nothing but an unbearable pain in her heart.

"Don't be ridiculous. This is what I get paid to do," he said.

"Then it's a stupid job." Her gaze met his, anger sparking between them mixing with the fear in an explosive combination. "As far as I'm concerned, you're fired."

"Sorry, but I don't work for you."

"That's right. You work for my father." She turned to run back to the lodge but he grabbed her arm and spun her into him. Her body slammed against his, knocking the breath out of her even before his mouth dropped to hers and his arms wrapped around her.

The kiss was all passion and fire, fear and regret. She'd seen the way he'd looked at her last night at the pool. The kiss took the rest of her breath. She leaned into him, letting him take her weight as she lost herself in his lips. His arms bound her to him as if he never wanted to let her go.

The sound of an approaching snowmobile droned loudly, bringing them both back from that amazing place the kiss had taken them.

His arms loosened but his mouth stayed on hers until the last possible moment. They parted just an instant before a snowmobile came roaring up over the rise in the trail.

She saw Chance's hand slip inside his coat to where she knew he'd holstered his weapon only minutes before. The snowmobile slowed, the rider's features ghostly behind the smoked glass of his helmet. He gave a nod and throttled the machine up as he zoomed past in a clatter of engine and cloud of gray smoke.

Dixie felt weak, as if it had taken all her energy to stand after what had just happened between her and Chance. Hadn't she always dreamed of this day? Not that it had happened as she'd hoped. No, nothing about this was how she'd imagined it.

Like the way he was looking at her now. As if he was mentally kicking himself for what he'd just done.

"Don't," she said, shaking her head. "Don't try to take that back. You messed up big-time not coming in the pool with me last night and we both know it. Don't make it worse by telling yourself you're sorry about that kiss."

He chuckled, his lips turning up in a grin. "You think you know what I'm feeling right now?" He shook his head. "I shouldn't have kissed you, but believe me I have no regrets."

She smiled. "Then I guess we're making progress."

"It's not going to happen again," he said, taking a step back as if he feared being too close to her.

She laughed. "We'll see."

"We need to talk about what just happened."

"I thought we were."

"Someone just *shot* at you," he said, way too serious.

"It isn't the first time. I told you, they shot at me in Texas as I was getting away."

He sighed as he raked a hand through his hair, his gaze locked with hers. "You're taking this awfully well."

She shook her head. "Don't you know me well enough by now to understand that I'm not one of those women who falls apart? When this is over…" She grinned. "Well, that will be another story. Right now, I just need to get to my aunt's before whoever took a shot at me does."

"You're right."

Her smile widened as she looked at him. "You should say that more often. I really like the sound of it."

"You know this doesn't necessarily mean that your father is behind this. It could be someone close to him. Someone he confides in. Or even someone who's put a tap on his phone line."

She cut her eyes to him. "Why are you defending him?"

"I just don't like jumping to conclusions," he said.

"No, you can't imagine a father wanting his daughter dead." She saw that she'd struck more than a nerve. "Will you tell me about your daughter some time?"

He reared back in surprise, shaking his head, his gaze warning her not to push this.

She took a breath, still trembling inside from her

encounter both with a near bullet wound—and her even more intimate encounter with Chance Walker. At this point, she would have been hard-pressed to say which had the most affect on her.

"That offer of a ride still open? Because my not-so-scrawny behind is freezing."

Chance looked relieved and maybe a little surprised that she'd dropped the subject so easily. Clearly he'd hoped she didn't know. He'd underestimated her. But then, he had from the start. Since the day Chance Walker had left Texas, she'd made a point of keeping up with his life in Montana. She was her father's daughter, after all.

CHANCE SAID NOTHING on the ride back to the lodge. On entering their suite, he picked up the phone, then put it back down again.

"You aren't going to call the police?" she asked, relieved.

He looked at her and she could tell he was struggling with this. "It isn't because I'm worried that your father's money has corrupted the local sheriff."

"So let me get this straight," she said. "There are times that it's a *bad* idea to call the cops?"

He scowled at her. "The sheriff would have to drive out for our statements. It would take hours. He'd check the tracks in the snow and find what I did. Man-size boot prints, nothing distinguishing about them. He would find the slug in the tree and figure out that it came from a rifle. He would trail the footprints to tire tracks."

She nodded.

Chance sighed. "In the end, he'd make the report and conclude it was probably a stray bullet from a late hunt."

"A hunter? You believe that?"

"No." He met her gaze and shook his head. "I still don't know what to believe."

She nodded, knowing the feeling only too well. "I meant what I said earlier. Call my father and quit. I don't want your death on my conscience."

"You have a conscience?"

"I'm serious, Chance."

He shook his head. "Sorry, but you didn't hire me, so you can't fire me. I'm in this to the end now."

"If it's the money—"

"It's not the money," he said, eyes snapping. "I finish what I start."

She cocked her head at him and grinned. "Really? That's good to hear." She hoped that also applied to what he'd started on the trail earlier.

"I mean it, Dixie. We're going to Livingston to talk to Glendora Ferris. I'm not finished until we find out who's trying to kill you and why."

She looked into his eyes and saw that he did mean it. "I just don't want you to be sorry."

He laughed. "Hell, I was sorry the minute I laid eyes on your father again. The way I see it, things can only get worse."

She wasn't sure how to take that since his gaze went to her lips as if he was remembering the kiss.

Unconsciously she touched the tip of her tongue to her upper lip. He groaned and turned away, leaving her smiling.

"Strip out of those wet clothes," he ordered, his back to her. "While you get a hot shower, I'll get your clothing dried. We'll stop by your car on the way to Livingston and get the rest of your clothes."

She stripped down and tossed her wet, cold clothing on the floor right behind him. He didn't move until she went into the bathroom and started to close the door. What was he so afraid of? But she knew the answer to that.

She turned on the shower and stepped under the spray, her skin red and chilled. She wrapped her arms around herself and stood under the hot water, thinking about Chance Walker, thinking about his daughter, and finally thinking about what had happened in the woods.

For a while, flirting with Chance, she'd been able to put it out of her mind. Hadn't she known that Chance had alerted the killers where she was by calling her father from the lodge phone?

Tears stung her eyes. What was it she'd stumbled across digging in her family's past that could make her own father want her dead?

Chapter Eleven

While Dixie was in the shower, Chance put in a call to Bonner in Texas and wasn't surprised when his call was answered by an abrupt, "Don't tell me you no longer have Dixie."

"Call off your thugs," Chance ordered.

"I told you I didn't hire anyone else."

"Bull."

"Chance, if there is anyone else after Dixie…well, I don't know anything about it. Have you asked *her?*"

"Listen, Bonner, someone just took a potshot at your daughter. I want to know what the hell is going on."

Bonner swore. "She's all right?"

"For the moment."

"You sure she isn't behind it? I wouldn't put anything past her—even setting up getting shot at to get you on her side."

"Her side? What the hell does that mean?"

"Just that Dixie gets things into her head—"

"Like trying to find her mother's relatives?" Chance asked.

Silence. "So she told you."

"Why don't you want her finding out about her mother's family? What are you afraid she's going to uncover?"

"I didn't even know Sarah *had* any relatives that were still alive and that's the truth. I just don't want Dixie digging into things that should stay in the past."

"Too late for that. Wanna tell me what in the past you're afraid is going to come out?"

"I told you there isn't any—"

Chance swore. "Did you go over to her house?"

"Just because the place was messed up doesn't mean Dixie didn't do it herself."

"For hell's sake, get your head out of the sand. Dixie's in trouble. If I find out you have anything to do with someone shooting—"

"She's my *daughter.* If anyone should know how a man feels about his daughter, it should be you."

"I mean it," Chance said, ignoring Bonner's last remark. "I won't rest until I see you behind bars if I find out you are in any way involved with trying to harm her."

GLENDORA FERRIS LIVED in a four-story white clapboard apartment house a few blocks from downtown Livingston.

The drive hadn't taken long from White Sulphur Springs. Chance had put country-western music on the radio and Dixie had dozed, too nervous to let herself think about what they might find once they reached Livingston.

Now, in the shadow of a massive peak, Dixie climbed out of the pickup to look up at the apartment house. Wind buffeted her hair and whirled snow around her.

Christmas lights strung across the front slapped the side of the apartment house to the rhythm of the gusts.

The house was old and in poor shape, paint peeling, the boards of the porch sagging and cracked. Faded curtains hung in what windows she could see from the front. She wondered if Glendora Ferris was watching them from behind one of those curtains.

As they started up the steps, clouds hung low over the town, the light flat, the wind icy-cold, as if another snowstorm was moving in. In the lobby, Dixie glanced at the decrepit elevator. It was small and dark and smelled of cooked cabbage.

She headed for the stairs. Chance didn't argue. As she recalled, he didn't like small, tight spaces any more than she did. The cab of the pickup had been intimate enough. She secretly suspected he liked having Beauregard the dog between them.

Because of Montana's higher altitude and the climb up four floors, Dixie felt winded by the time they reached Glendora Ferris's apartment. Dixie waited a few seconds to catch her breath, knowing part of her hesitancy was fear. She was depending on this woman being her aunt. On finding answers behind this door.

At her knock came the sound of an older female voice on the other side. "Just a minute."

Dixie wiped her palms down the sides of her jeans, jittery with nerves, and glanced at Chance. He gave her an encouraging nod. He was the one person who knew how much was riding on this. Finally, she might get the answers she so desperately needed.

She warned herself not to get her hopes up, but it was

too late for that. She couldn't help her excitement as the door opened a crack and a weathered face peered out between the door and chain.

Dixie looked into a pair of watery-blue eyes. "Glendora?"

The woman blinked. "Yes?"

"My name is Dixie Bonner. My mother was Sarah Worth?"

"Elizabeth?" The door closed.

Dixie looked over at Chance. *Elizabeth?* The chain grated in the latch. The door opened again.

The woman standing in front of them was anywhere from her seventies to late eighties. She wore a faded housecoat. Her hands were boney-thin and flecked with age spots. But it was the expression she wore that made Dixie's heart take a nosedive.

The woman looked totally lost, her gray hair poking up at all angles, her eyes blank. "Elizabeth?" She was looking around as if she'd expected someone else.

"I'm the daughter of Sarah Worth," Dixie said, bringing the woman's attention back to her. "I'm looking for her sister Glendora?"

"Elizabeth?" The woman didn't move, but her body began to quiver and she reached for the doorjamb as if needing it for support. Dixie moved quickly to her, putting an arm around the frail shoulders and leading her back inside to the couch.

"I'm sorry. I didn't mean to upset you," Dixie said, patting the woman's boney hand as she lowered her to the couch.

Behind them, Chance stepped in and closed the door.

The poor woman had no idea who Dixie was.

"Can I get you some water?" Dixie offered, glancing toward the kitchenette.

The woman shook her head, never taking her eyes off Dixie. "I thought you were a ghost." She reached out to take Dixie's hand, pulling her down beside her on the couch. "You look so much like her. Elizabeth isn't with you?"

"Elizabeth?" Dixie asked, fighting her disappointment. This woman wasn't going to be of any help.

"Elizabeth." She seemed unaware of the tears on her translucent cheeks. "That was her real name. Sarah was her *middle* name."

Dixie stared at the woman in shock. "Then, you're her sister Glendora?"

The woman smiled. "What did you say your name was?"

"Dixie."

"Dixie." She looked confused again. "I thought her daughter's name was Rebecca?"

Relief washed over Dixie. She laughed. "My older sister's name is Rebecca."

"Elizabeth had more children?" Glendora sounded surprised by that. Almost disapproving. She still hadn't seemed to notice Chance waiting by the door.

"I lost track of Elizabeth after she had her little girl," Glendora said, then lowered her voice as if the walls had ears. "I couldn't understand how she could have two babies with that man. I guess things must have gotten better since she had you. You did say your name was Bonner, right?"

Dixie nodded. "You didn't like her husband?"

"Husband?" Glendora huffed. "He didn't want anything to do with marriage. I never saw him shed a tear for his *own* son when he died." She wagged her head. "Elizabeth was so young, so innocent. She didn't know that some men are scoundrels. I tried to warn her about him. I was six years older, more like a mother to her since we'd lost our parents and lived with a maiden aunt."

Dixie listened, trying to imagine her mother, young and naive, falling for a scoundrel.

"She was so heartbroken when she lost her son. I suppose that's why she wanted another baby. That, and to try to hang on to that man." Glendora's expression softened as she reached out to touch Dixie's face. "You look just like her. Is she still..."

Dixie shook her head. "She died when I was thirteen months old."

Glendora's watery eyes filled with tears. "I guess I always knew that she wasn't long for this world. She was too good." She met Dixie's gaze. "She was still with him?"

"Yes," Dixie said.

"I heard he moved her to Texas to work some farm."

The Bonner farm. Was it possible oil hadn't been discovered on the land yet? "So she had the baby boy in...?"

"Idaho, where we lived." She scowled. "Only lived a few weeks."

"Then my brother is buried in Idaho?"

"Ashton." She was staring at Dixie again, her eyes brimming with tears.

"What did she name him?" Dixie asked.

"Beauregard Bonner Junior Worth," Glendora said.

No wonder Dixie hadn't found him. She'd never dreamed her mother hadn't been married yet.

"I never knew what happened to my sister once she went to Texas. He didn't like her having anyone but him." She glanced toward the door and seemed to see Chance for the first time. "You have a handsome husband."

Dixie didn't correct her. "I never knew my father was ever in Idaho." She'd heard her uncle Carl and Mason and Ace all talk about their adventures. Her father hadn't always stayed in Texas, but he'd never said where he'd been. She thought she now knew why.

Strange, though, that he'd never mentioned that was where he'd met her mother. Or that they'd had a son who died up there and then had Rebecca before moving back to Texas.

All to hide the fact that he hadn't married her yet?

Is that why he'd flatly denied knowing the people in the photographs? She'd known he was lying, but she couldn't understand how or why he would lie about his own son and daughter, no matter the situation.

"There must have been something about my father that made her fall in love with him," Dixie said.

"Oh, he was smooth. Cocky and full of himself. Swept Elizabeth off her feet with all his grandiose plans. Did he ever make anything of himself?"

"Not really," Dixie said, and heard Chance chuckle where he leaned against the wall by the door.

She glanced around the small apartment. "Is there any chance you have a photograph of my mother?"

Glendora looked toward the back of the apartment, her expression vague. "I had some. Let me see if I can find them." She pushed herself up from the couch and disappeared into the bedroom.

Dixie looked over at Chance. She knew what he must be thinking. Why would anyone want to kill her over any of this? It made no sense. There was no mystery here. No deep, dark secret unless it was the fact that Rebecca had been born out of wedlock. Wouldn't Rebecca have a fit if she knew.

"Sounds like your father has a few secrets," Chance said.

She nodded, thinking this would explain why she'd had trouble finding out anything about her mother given that her mother's real name apparently wasn't Sarah, but Elizabeth Sarah Worth and she was born in Idaho—not Texas.

Glendora returned with a rubber-banded shoe box. She set it on the coffee table in front of the couch. "There might be something in here. I've moved so much, a lot of things have been lost over the years."

Dixie slipped off the rubber band and lifted the lid on the shoe box as Glendora joined her on the couch again.

The box was filled with black-and-white photos, the edges rough, the paper yellowed and curled.

She looked up at Chance, then with trembling fingers reached into the box and began to go through the photos.

Glendora couldn't remember most of the names of the people in the snapshots. "It's been too long," she said.

Dixie looked for a face that resembled her own, given that she'd been told she looked like her mother. The deeper she dug in the box, though, the more disappointed she became. Most of the photographs, it turned out, were from Glendora's first husband's family.

"You're so lucky to have a sister," Glendora said. "I wished my sister and I could have stayed together."

Dixie nodded, feeling guilty since she and Rebecca had never been close even though they now lived only a few miles from each other. "Would you like me to send you some photographs? Rebecca has three children."

Glendora smiled, her eyes misty. "I would love that."

Dixie picked up a photograph of a cute little girl with long blond hair making a face at the camera.

"That's Amelia," Glendora said, and reached for the photograph, smiling as she studied the girl's face.

"Amelia?"

"Amelia Hardaway. She married the oldest McCarthy boy." Glendora fell silent and Dixie could see that all this was tiring her. She quickly dug through the rest of the photographs, holding out little hope any of her mother had survived.

Glendora was still clutching the photo of the little girl. "Amelia was your mother's best friend. Those two…" she said, as if lost in the past. "They were inseparable."

Dixie could feel Chance's gaze on her. "Is Amelia still around?"

"I got a Christmas card. Was it this year or last?" She frowned as if trying to remember. "She didn't get far from home. Still lives on the farm outside of Ashton. Or she did. I think she said her husband died."

Dixie turned one of the last photographs over and froze. It was of two young girls, one about eleven, the other in her late teens.

Her heart took off in a gallop as she stared into the face of the younger girl. She felt Chance's palm on her back and looked up, and realized she must have made a sound that brought him to the end of the couch next to her.

She showed the snapshot to Glendora, not wanting to let go of it. "Is that you and my mother?"

Glendora smiled and nodded, eyes misting over. "My baby sister."

Dixie quickly looked through the few remaining photographs, finding only one other one of her mother. In it, both girls were older. Glendora was standing next to a bus, a suitcase at her feet. Beside Glendora was her younger sister holding a baby and next to Dixie's mother was a man wearing a fedora, his face in shadow and turned away from the camera as if he didn't want his photo taken.

"That was the day I left home," Glendora said, leaning in to look at the snapshot. "My aunt took the photo of all of us. It was the last time I saw Elizabeth and Rebecca. Our aunt died a few years later, but Elizabeth didn't come back for the funeral."

Dixie stared at the photo, running her finger over her mother's face. There was definitely a resemblance between her and her mother at this age. She could understand now why sometimes she caught her father looking at her with such a sad expression.

"Who is the man standing next to my mother?" Dixie asked.

Glendora looked up at her in surprise. "Why that's your

father. He was a lot younger then, but that's him, all right. Beauregard Bonner. Like I could ever forget that name."

Dixie stared at the man in the photo. It was definitely not Beauregard Bonner.

Chapter Twelve

Chance felt as shaken as Dixie looked as they left Glendora's apartment. "You all right?" he asked once they were outside.

Dixie nodded, seemingly afraid to trust her voice. He watched her breathe in the cold air, taking huge gulps.

He knew that everything was finally starting to catch up with her. Saying nothing, he put his arm around her and pulled her close as they walked to the pickup. Beauregard was fogging up the window watching them. Tiny snowflakes glittered suspended in the air. Across the street, a gust of wind whirled snow across a yard, knocking over a huge plastic Santa Claus.

Dixie had the two photographs gripped in her fingers. She protectively stuck them in her purse as he rushed to open her door and shoo Beauregard over.

Chance saw her glance up at the fourth-floor window before she climbed in. He shut her door and ran around to his side, still trying to make sense of what Glendora had told them.

As he slid behind the wheel, Dixie took the

photographs from her purse and looked at them again. He started the truck, pretty sure he knew where they were headed next, but first he wanted something hot to drink and food wasn't a bad idea, either.

He found a café next to the old train depot. The lunch crowd had already cleared out so the place was practically empty. They took a booth at the back.

"Food," Dixie said as she sat.

Chance laughed. "I should have known that would be the first word out of your mouth."

They ordered the lunch special. Dixie laid the photographs on the table as gently as if they were made of glass.

"Who is he?" she asked, looking up at Chance, her eyes blank as if in shock.

"Glendora could be wrong."

Clearly, Dixie didn't believe that any more than he did. "That man, whoever he is, fathered a son who died, then Rebecca. That means that Rebecca is my *half* sister. We didn't have the same father." Dixie seemed blown away by that thought. "It would explain why we are so different."

He still didn't know what to make of any of this. "The obvious answer would be that Glendora is wrong about the man in the photograph. He could have just been a friend of the family."

"I might believe that if my father hadn't tried so hard to talk me out of searching for the people in the photographs I found."

"Okay," he said. "But then, where does your father fit in all of this?"

"I don't know and that's what worries me," she said,

and glanced out at the darkening sky over Sheep Mountain. She reached into her bag and took out her cell phone. "There is only one way to find out."

"Are you sure that's a good idea?" Chance asked as she pulled on her coat and rose from the booth.

"Are you kidding? At this point, I'm not sure anything is a good idea." She waited as if needing his encouragement.

"Maybe he'll clear everything up."

She shook her head at him in wonder. "You slay me. Maybe he'll call off whoever he's hired to kill me and tell me the truth. Right." She turned on her heel and headed for the door as she keyed in the number and put the phone to her ear.

Chance watched her go, wishing he could spare her this conversation because no matter what Beauregard Bonner told his daughter, he had a bad feeling she wasn't going to like it.

DIXIE STEPPED just outside the café, leaning against the building out of the wind. A banner flapped loudly nearby. Snow blew past in swirling white gusts. She stared down the train tracks as the phone rang.

"Hello?"

Just the sound of her father's voice stopped her cold. She felt tears burn her eyes. She flashed on Christmas mornings when she was a child and saw her father excitedly handing out presents.

They always got way too much, but it was his delight at being able to give them everything they wanted that she thought about now. She couldn't remember the last time they'd all had Christmas together and the thought filled her with sadness. Had she changed? Or her father?

"Hello?" He sounded ready to hang up.

She swallowed hard, the wind whistling past her. "It's Dixie."

Silence. Then, "Are you all right?"

"That's hard to answer."

"Isn't Chance there?"

She smiled at that. "I haven't given him the slip, if that's what you're asking. I need to ask you about my mother and this time I need you to be honest with me."

He made a sound, a groan, then she heard a chair creak as he sat down. "Dixie…"

"I found my aunt Glendora. My mother's sister. Aren't you going to say anything?"

"Your mother told me she was an only child," he said, his voice soft, almost sad. "Her parents were deceased."

"I know about Rebecca."

"Dixie…" The sadness of that one word told her he wasn't going to deny that Rebecca wasn't his. "Dixie, come home so we can talk about this."

"We could have talked about it when I showed you the photographs I found in my mother's jewelry box," she snapped. "Instead you lied and said they didn't even belong to our family and that you would get rid of them for me."

"I should have told you then, but I was so shocked to see that she'd kept photographs…" His voice broke. "I knew your mother had been in love with another man. The man abandoned her. She had a baby girl with him."

"She had two children with him. The first one, a boy, died when he was a few weeks old."

A strangled sound. "I didn't know. She never told me." He sounded heartbroken. Was it possible he was telling the truth?

"If you had just been honest with me…"

"I never wanted your sister to know. She was *my* daughter. I raised her from the time she was just a child. I *loved* her just as I loved you." He sounded as if he was crying. "You're my girls."

She felt the tug on her heartstrings so strong it made her legs weak. How could she believe he was trying to have her killed? He was her *father*. "Who was the man?"

He blew his nose, cleared his throat. "I don't know. Honestly. She never told me."

"You never asked about my sister's father?"

"I didn't want to know. He'd abandoned Sarah when she'd needed him the most. What kind of man does that?"

What kind of man does *anything* to keep the past from surfacing? "Dad—" her voice broke "—how far would you go to keep me from finding out the truth?"

"Dixie, what are you talking about?"

"Someone is trying to kill me and now that you're trying to get into politics…"

"Dixie, you can't believe that I—"

"I saw the men who grabbed me. One of them works for you."

Beauregard Bonner let out a curse. "Dixie, if that's true, tell me who he is. I'll get to the bottom of this—"

"I don't know his name. But I've seen him at Bonner Unlimited. He might have been one of the security guards at the main desk."

"And you decided because of that, he was working for me?" her father demanded, sounding angry and hurt. "Damn it, Dixie, he might have been fired and just wanted to get even with me. I don't personally hire any of those men and you know it."

"What matters is that the men were after my research on the family. I heard them when they were ransacking my house looking for my journal."

"Dixie, I don't know what's going on, but you're scaring me. Please. Come home so I can keep you safe here. The jet will be there tomorrow. Meet me there. Please."

She made a swipe at her tears as she glanced back into the café. The waitress was putting her order on the table. "I have to go."

"Tell me you'll be at the plane. You know I'd move heaven and earth to keep you safe, don't you?"

"That why you hired Chance?" she asked.

"I knew I could trust him. He won't let anything happen to you."

She closed her eyes. "This other man that my mother was in love with...he called himself Beauregard Bonner."

"*What?* It wasn't me. You have to believe me."

"I do believe you. It might be the only thing I believe that you've told me. I saw an old photograph of the man. It wasn't you. I have to go." She snapped off the phone, her hand trembling. Tears burned her eyes. She stood, huddled against the wind, afraid to let herself believe her father. Afraid he'd do more than disappoint her.

BEAUREGARD HAD JUST HUNG up when he realized he wasn't alone. He spun around, half expecting it would be his worthless son-in-law. He was only partially relieved to see that it was Mason.

"What? First I find you in my office when I'm not here and now you just walk in without knocking," Beau snapped.

Mason held up both hands. "The door was open. Since when do I have to knock anyway?" He stepped in, closing the door behind him. "Tell me what's happened that has you biting my head off?"

Beau leaned back in his chair, feeling more exhausted than he'd ever been before. "I'm sorry. I just got a call from Dixie. She found some photographs in her mother's jewelry box and has been trying to find the people in the snapshots."

Mason took a chair. "Snapshots?"

"Sarah had a sister, apparently."

Mason looked surprised. "I thought you said she was an only child."

"Apparently not."

"Is Dixie sure about this? I mean, why wouldn't Sarah have told you?"

Beau shook his head. "There is a lot Sarah didn't tell me. She had another child with the man. A son who died."

"This is what Dixie's been doing? Why would she drag all this up knowing how much it hurts you?" Mason was on his feet, pacing the floor.

"I should have told her when I saw the photographs from Sarah's jewelry box. If I had been honest with her—"

"Like that would have stopped Dixie." Mason shook his head irritably. "This is all Carl's fault. He had to give her that damned jewelry box…"

"Carl couldn't have known the photographs were in it. They were hidden under the velvet lining, Dixie said. They'd been there for years."

Mason swung around. "Didn't Carl know? Damn it, Beau, he resents the hell out of you. He's not even your real brother."

Beauregard felt as if he'd been touched with a live wire. The shock ricocheted through him, taking his breath. "I never want to hear you say that again. Do you hear me?" He was on his feet. "Carl *is* my brother. I don't give a damn if the old man denied it. He's my *brother.* Just as Rebecca and Dixie are sisters."

Mason raised a brow. "That's what you're really afraid Dixie's going to find out, isn't it? You feel guilty because the old man left everything to you. Didn't leave a cent to his first son. You got rich. And Carl…well, Carl gets a free ride. Not quite the same as being the son his father loved though, is it?"

Beau could feel his blood pressure soaring. "I won't hear another word about this. Especially from a man who doesn't even know who his father was."

Mason looked stunned and Beau instantly regretted his words. "I'm sorry."

Mason waved the apology away. "You're upset. I understand that. I just hate to see you get hurt any worse,

Beau." He stepped to the bar and poured them both a drink. Mason had a knack for calming him down. "I didn't mean to set you off, but damn it, Beau, you have to know what's at stake here."

Oh hell, yes, he knew. He'd known since the day his father died and left him what Earle Bonner thought was nothing but a worthless Texas farm with a dirty flea-ridden shack on it.

"Don't you think Carl suspects you knew about the oil before the old man died?" Mason asked quietly as he handed him a drink and took his own to a chair. "Hell, I've always had the feeling he's been waiting for the day he could even the score with not just you, but me, as well."

"Carl has nothing to do with this," Beau said as he cradled the drink in his hands without taking a sip. He'd been drinking too much lately. He had to slow down, get his head clear.

"You remember the story of Cain and Abel from that summer at Bible school?" Mason asked. "Carl has always been jealous of you. You think that doesn't eat away at a man over the years. Your old man denied Carl's parentage and treated him like the bastard he was while you could do nothing wrong. If Carl saw a chance to even the score, you telling me he wouldn't take advantage of it?"

"Mason, please," Beau said, too tired to argue.

Mason downed his drink, sighed and took his glass to the sink at the bar. As he started to leave, he stopped to place a hand on Beau's shoulder. "I'm your oldest friend. If I step over the line sometimes, I'm sorry, but you know I have your best interests at heart and always have. I told you not to hire Carl or that no-good cousin of yours."

"What has Ace done now?" Beau asked, although he didn't really want to know.

"Didn't show for work all week, but apparently got an advance on his wages," Mason said. "Beau, you can't throw money at people to placate them. It only makes them more bitter. Ask my ex-wife if you don't believe me." He paused. "I'll call you when I get back in a few days."

Beau looked at him in surprise.

"You do remember that I'll be out of town on business?" Mason was frowning. "You told me to take the small jet? Beau, don't tell me—"

"Sure, sure," Beau said. "It just slipped my mind." He didn't remember but he'd had a lot on his mind lately. He wondered what business, but didn't ask, not wanting Mason to know just how forgetful he'd been lately.

"Are you sure you're all right?" Mason asked. "Maybe I should put this off—"

"No, you go ahead. I'm fine. Please. Dixie will be flying home tomorrow. I can handle things here."

Mason hesitated, but had the good sense to leave without another word.

The moment he was gone, Beau put down his drink and rubbed his forehead. He was getting another headache. He'd had a lot of them lately. That was probably another reason he was having trouble remembering things. He'd also been misplacing things. It was the strain of running a company this size.

But in truth he knew what was bothering him. He closed his eyes, thinking about what Mason had said.

He thought about his brother Carl. Mason didn't understand their relationship. Carl didn't care about his birthright as the oldest son. He'd hated the farm. And hated their father.

Beau felt a chill as he recalled the day their father died. Both of their mothers had been gone for years. Beau had come back to the farm to help. Carl had, too, after years of kicking around the country.

That day, Beau had come into the house to see Carl coming out of the old man's room. Carl had a funny expression on his face. "He's gone," Carl had said to Beau. "The devil has him now." And Beau had thought Carl had been fighting tears as he'd come out of the room. But the truth was, Carl had been smiling.

CHANCE NOTICED THAT Dixie hadn't come right back into the café after her phone call with her father. He'd watched her through the window, reading her body language, knowing how upset she was. He was just getting ready to go out to see if she was all right when she opened the door and came toward him.

Now as he saw her face, he knew it had gone better than maybe she'd hoped. She seemed stronger. Or, at least, she was giving it her best show. With Dixie, he never knew.

"He says he doesn't know who the man was," she said, sliding into the booth and picking up her fork. "He swears my mother told him she was an orphan with no siblings."

Chance nodded. "Maybe he didn't know the people in the photographs, then. Your mother probably didn't tell him about her sister because it was all tied to that other man and the past."

She shrugged and took a bite of the lunch special. He

suspected she wouldn't even be able to taste it in the mood she was in.

Chance checked his cell phone, not surprised to find a message from Bonner. He listened to it, a command to call. He looked at Dixie, then put the cell phone away.

"You aren't going to call him?" she asked.

"I'll call him when I know what's going on," he said. He knew Bonner would want details, as well as a promise that Dixie would be at the plane tomorrow. Chance couldn't make that promise right now and he figured telling Bonner wasn't going to help matters.

"He says he's not hiding anything and denies he would ever hurt me."

"And if he's telling the truth?"

She looked at him, her eyes misting over. "I was thinking about that. Who else has something to lose besides my father? Who else wouldn't want the truth coming out?"

He saw where she was headed. "The man in the photograph."

She nodded. "He could have his own reasons for not wanting me to find out who he is. Look at the way he has his face turned away from the camera, as if he didn't want his picture taken."

Chance nodded. "You're saying he somehow found out that you were trying to find your mother's relatives and he's the one who's been trying to stop you?"

She nodded as she cupped her hands around her coffee mug, clearly needing the warmth.

"You do know what that would mean," he said.

"Since one of the men who tried to kill me works for

my father—or at least, used to—that would mean that the man is connected to Bonner Unlimited. Maybe even close to my father."

"Given the fact that the man used your father's name more than thirty years ago, I'd say he not only knows your father but has known him for a long time," Chance said.

"You think he might have been blackmailing my father so the truth didn't come out about Rebecca?"

Chance shook his head. "Your father would never have bowed to blackmail."

"Even if he knew that the news would kill my sister? You know how Rebecca is. She cares more about what those snob friends of hers think about her than anything in this world. Even her money and possessions. All that is just to impress them, to get them to accept her. Imagine if it came out that she's not even a Bonner?"

He could imagine that. He could imagine even worse. "This man sounds pretty unsavory."

Dixie nodded, tears in her eyes. "I'm sorry I ever opened this Pandora's box. Rebecca will be devastated when she finds out."

"That would have given the man motive for blackmail," Chance agreed. "Maybe that's why your father is so desperate to get you back to Montana where he can protect you from this person because he does know how dangerous the man is."

Dixie looked thoughtful. "That's why we need to find out who—" A freight train roared past within feet of where they sat. The café windows rattled loudly, making being heard impossible. It wasn't until the train was long past that she could finish "—who the man is in the photograph."

Dixie picked up the snapshot again, studying it in the light. "It's too bad it's not a better photograph. With his face in shadow…" She handed it over to him and watched as he inspected it.

"Add to that the fact that this was taken at least thirty years ago," Chance said, thinking out loud. The man was tall and lanky, young, maybe late teens or early twenties. It was hard to tell. "Who knows what he looks like now."

"It still doesn't explain why someone wants me dead," Dixie said as they ate, and made an attempt to lighten the conversation. "Unless Rebecca took out a contract on me so I wouldn't tell her friends in Houston society."

"There's nothing quite like sibling rivalry."

Dixie laughed.

He was glad to see her smile. She really did have a great smile.

"If Rebecca is behind it, though, I don't know why she wasted her money on hit men," Dixie continued. "She should have tried to bribe me first."

"Like she has anything *you* want," he said, joining in.

When she didn't say anything, he looked up from his plate to see her staring at him, her face deadly serious.

"She had you," Dixie said.

Joking or not, he wasn't going there. He was having trouble thinking of her as Rebecca's little sister. Dixie was a beautiful woman and he would have been a fool to pretend he hadn't noticed. And he wasn't that big of a fool.

Or maybe he was, he thought, remembering kissing her. Not that he regretted the kiss. What he couldn't do was get distracted. Too much was at stake. Someone had shot at Dixie this morning. He couldn't keep kidding himself that her life wasn't in danger. He'd been hired to find her and to keep her safe, and he always did what he was hired to do.

That is, he always had. Unfortunately, he was starting to realize that he might break that rule tomorrow when Bonner sent a private jet to pick up his daughter in Helena.

Unless Chance could be sure Dixie would be safe returning to Texas, then there was no way he was letting her near that plane.

DIXIE WATCHED CHANCE out of the corner of her eye as he ordered them pie for dessert. Banana cream, her favorite.

"You realize this is the first thing we had in common," she said.

He glanced up, his fork loaded with pie partway to his mouth. "What?"

"You and me," she said. "We both loved to eat. Remember those nights when you would bring Rebecca home from a date and the cook would have just baked cookies or a pie or one of those chocolate-covered cherry cakes with the really thick fudge icing?"

He laughed and nodded as he took a bite of his pie.

"You and I would sit in the kitchen and talk and eat while Rebecca searched the fridge for celery or tofu or carrot sticks." She made a face remembering how Rebecca was always on a diet even though she'd never been even close to fat.

"I think my favorite was your cook's buttermilk pie. Remember it?" he asked.

She rolled her eyes as if in ecstasy. "Oh, I'd forgotten all about that pie."

They talked of food and laughed about some of the late-night conversations they'd had discussing everything from religion to space aliens and crop circles.

When they'd finished their desserts, they walked out to the pickup in a companionable silence. Chance tensed, though, his hand staying close to the weapon strapped under his coat and his gaze taking in everything around them as they left the café.

It wasn't until they were safe in the pickup that he said, "I used to really enjoy those talks with you. You were pretty smart for twelve."

"Thanks. I think." Dixie spotted a bell ringer in front of one of the shops. He was dressed as Santa. On impulse, she reached into her purse, dug around and pulled out the diamond ring Roy Bob Jackson had left in her Christmas stocking. She ran across the street to drop the ring in the man's pot, then ran back to the pickup.

She climbed in, giving Beauregard the treat she'd brought him, most of her Salisbury steak from her lunch special. He gobbled it down and curled up against her leg. She put her hand on his big soft furry head and waited for Chance to start the engine. She could feel his gaze on her.

"Ol' Roy Bob won't be happy about that," Chance said.

"No, he won't," she said, and grinned. "That ring was worth about fifty grand. So we're going to Ashton?"

"Was there ever any doubt?"

"Thank you, but could I ask one favor? Could we stop back by Glendora's? I want to ask her more about the man in the photograph. I was so shocked before, I didn't know what to say."

Chance agreed it was a good idea. Maybe Glendora might remember something about the man that would help.

Where did her father fit into all this? Or did he? Maybe he was telling the truth and he hadn't known anything about her mother's past. But then, why was he so afraid for Dixie? What was it he still feared she would find out? The name of her mother's lover?

Dixie took in the small western town, her own fears gripping her as Chance drove down the main drag. Livingston sat in a hole, hemmed in by the Yellowstone River and the mountains. Wind whipped an American flag, the edge frayed, and sent snow skittering across the pavement.

She could feel the cold just outside the pickup window. She snuggled against Chance's warm, big dog, telling herself it was too late to quit. Even if she decided to stop looking for answers now, she doubted it would stop whoever was after her.

A chill rippled through her as they neared Glendora's apartment house that had nothing to do with the cold winter day. She heard sirens.

Chapter Thirteen

Chance heard the sirens just an instant before he saw the flashing lights. A cop car stopped next to an ambulance in front of Glendora's apartment house.

Dixie's face mirrored his own thoughts as he parked at the curb up the block from the house. A crowd had gathered on the sidewalk. Another police officer was directing traffic around the ambulance parked at the curb.

"It might not be Glendora," he said as they approached the scene, hoping to hell that was the case.

"Right," Dixie said, her voice breaking as she quickened her pace.

At the edge of the small crowd, Chance took her arm to hold her back. "Let me find out."

"What happened?" he asked an elderly woman in the crowd.

"One of the tenants. They say she fell down the stairs," the woman said.

"Who was it?" he asked.

The woman looked to a younger woman standing next to her. "An elderly woman who lived on the fourth floor. They said the elevator wasn't working and she must have tried to take the stairs."

Chance still had his hand on Dixie's arm and could feel her trembling. The wind whipped at their clothing and sent snow showering down on them as the ambulance attendants came out of the front door of the apartment house with the stretcher, the body in a black bag.

Chance let go of Dixie, stepped over to one of the policemen and flashed his credentials before asking the name of the deceased.

"Name's Glendora Ferris. A neighbor heard her fall down the stairs and called 9-1-1," the cop told him.

BEAU STOOD at his office window, waiting. He really did have one hell of a view.

"You wanted to see me?"

He turned to look at his brother standing in the office doorway. Carl was wearing a Western shirt, jeans, boots. His gray hair needed to be cut and his white Stetson cleaned. Carl Bonner looked nothing like the multimillionaire he was.

Beau instantly regretted calling his brother into the office. Mason was wrong. Carl had more money than he would ever use. Nor was he apt to dream up some lame kidnapping plot that had failed to get a million and a half out of Beau anymore than he would give Dixie the jewelry box hoping she would find the photographs inside.

Because that would mean that Carl knew about the photos. Knew about Sarah's past. And how was that possible?

"Thought you might like to join me in a drink," Beau said, and motioned his brother in.

"Little early for me," Carl said, but closed the door and entered the office. "What's up?"

Beau poured himself a Scotch, figuring he was going to need it. "I wanted to ask you about Dixie."

"Dixie?" Carl said, frowning.

"Have you seen her?"

"Not for a while. Is something wrong?"

Beau took his drink back to his desk and sat, motioning for Carl to do the same. "She's in Montana."

Carl's brows lifted as he took a seat. "What's she doing up there?"

"Trying to find out more about her mother's family," Beau said, sorry to hear his words edged with criticism.

Carl nodded. "Bound to happen."

Beau opened his mouth to argue the point and closed it. He didn't want to fight about this. "She found some photographs in that jewelry box you gave her."

Carl frowned. "Photographs?"

"Apparently from Sarah's life before me," Beau said. "You didn't know she kept them?"

"No. Did you?"

"What are you asking?" Carl said quietly.

What was he asking? What possible reason would Carl have for purposely giving Dixie her mother's jewelry box if he knew there were old photos hidden inside? None. Carl wouldn't want to hurt the girls. Not only that, Dixie'd had the jewelry box for years and had only just now found the photographs.

Beau rubbed his temples feeling a headache coming

on. "Never mind me. I'm just in a foul mood." He'd made the mistake of not telling Dixie the truth straight-away. Instead all he'd done was whet her curiosity and when Dixie got on the scent of what she thought was a secret, she was like a hound dog after a buried bone.

"Sarah had a sister," Beau said. "She never men-tioned it to me, but Dixie found out somehow."

Carl shook his head and said nothing.

"What?" Beau demanded.

"Nothing, it's just that you knew Sarah had a life before you."

"I didn't care about her past," Beau snapped, not wanting to admit that Sarah had lied to him. Maybe that's what hurt the most.

"I remember the night the two of you met," Carl said.

Beau felt all the air rush from him. He swallowed hard, picked up his drink and downed it. He'd forgot-ten about the first time he'd seen her.

CHANCE STARED UP at Glendora's apartment building windows as the body was loaded into the ambulance. Christmas lights strung across the front entry slapped the side of the house in the wind. A piece of newspaper blew by. Somewhere in the distance a horn honked, brakes squealed.

"Come on, let's get out of here," Chance said, steering Dixie toward the pickup, all the time watching the street and residences around them. For all he knew, the killer might be watching them at this very moment.

"You know she didn't fall down the stairs."

He could hear the anguish in her voice. The woman

had been her aunt. Dixie had promised to send pictures of Rebecca's children to her. He put his arm around her as they neared the pickup.

"I'm so sorry, but it could have been an accident. You heard them say the elevator wasn't working," he said.

Dixie shook off his arm and climbed into the pickup. As he slid behind the wheel, she snapped, "Do me a favor. Stop trying to protect me from the truth."

"I don't know what the truth is and neither do you," he said as he watched the crowd disassemble and the cops leave. "We probably will never know what really happened to her."

"I led a killer straight to her. I just as good as murdered her," Dixie said.

He looked over at her, seeing how hurt and angry and scared she was. "Dixie, this isn't your fault."

"If I hadn't found those photographs in my mother's jewelry box…"

"Your mother kept them obviously because she couldn't part with them and had no idea that someday you would find them and this would happen," he said. "What you're not considering is that the man in the photograph has known about Glendora for years."

"Maybe he didn't know where she was, though, until I led him to her."

Chance shook his head. "It doesn't make any sense. Why kill Glendora? What did she really know? That Rebecca was another man's child? She didn't even know the man's real name. The photos were gone. So why kill her? We'd already been there. She'd already told us everything she knew."

Dixie knew what he was saying was true. It didn't make any sense. She took the photographs from her purse and studied them again. "He's tying up all the loose ends, probably wishing he'd done it years ago. But now maybe he *has* to." She looked over at Chance. "For whatever reason, he is more desperate to keep that life a secret."

"To protect himself?" Chance asked. "Or someone else?"

She shook her head. "Rebecca's his illegitimate daughter. What if he doesn't want her to know who he is?"

"Maybe."

"And why did my mother change her name from Elizabeth Worth to Sarah Worth when she went to Texas?"

They had more questions than answers as Chance headed out of town, all the time watching his rearview mirror. They hadn't been followed to Livingston. He was sure of that. Just as they hadn't been followed to Glendora Ferris's apartment.

"I know you're going to think this is crazy," she said as she glanced behind them. "But I feel as if the man has more to lose now than ever before. He's determined to bury the past and me with it."

THE FIRST TIME Beau had seen Sarah Worth she'd been in the small café not far from the Bonner farm, sitting with Carl and Mason, talking.

He recalled how she'd looked up, their gazes meeting. Carl or Mason had introduced him.

"Beauregard Bonner?" She'd smiled as if she'd liked his name. Liked him.

Hell, he'd always told himself it was love at first sight. But now he knew that she was more than familiar with the name. Because her lover had been using it. Rebecca's real father.

"So did Sarah tell you anything about her baby's father that first night before I came in?" Beau asked his brother now, trying to keep the emotion out of his voice.

Carl shook his head.

"Damn it, Carl, if you know who he is…"

"Did you ask Mason?"

Beau stared at his brother. "You think she told Mason?"

Carl shrugged. "Mason's the one who bought her a cup of coffee and invited her over to our table."

"Mason has always been a womanizer." Sarah was a beautiful woman. What man wouldn't have been interested? He remembered how surprised he'd been when he'd seen the baby sleeping peacefully in the carrier on the chair next to her. He'd fallen in love with both of them. "I'm sure Mason lost interest the moment he realized she had a baby."

Carl shrugged again. "I saw Mason talking to Sarah quite a few times in town. Looked like pretty heated conversations."

"Come on, you were always talking to Sarah. Looked pretty serious at times." Beau regretted his words instantly. But he was sick to death of Mason and Carl constantly back-biting. They were more like brothers than Beau and Carl, jealous and convinced Beau liked one more than the other.

Carl was smiling now. "Sarah and I liked to talk about books. You were always busy trying to make more money. If you think I envied you because you had Sarah…" His smile broadened. "You're damn right I did. She was a fine woman and you were damned lucky that she loved you."

Beau felt even more like a heel. "I'm sorry."

"Look," Carl said reasonably, "Sarah's dead. What difference does any of this make now?"

"Because Dixie is determined to find out," Beau snapped. "I'm afraid for her. She's convinced that I hired someone to…kill her to keep her from learning the truth."

Carl raised a brow.

"You don't really think I would do that, do you?" Beau demanded. "All I can figure is that the man Sarah was with before me got wind of what Dixie was doing and doesn't want her digging in the past."

"Why do you think that?" Carl asked.

"Who else? I guess he doesn't want any of this coming out especially considering that when he was with Sarah he called himself Beauregard Bonner."

Carl laughed and shook his head. "Everyone always wanted to be Beauregard Bonner."

"Even you?" Beau asked.

Carl laughed harder. "Not a chance. I like being in the background, out of the line of fire. But it would explain how Sarah came to this part of Texas. Otherwise it is one hell of a coincidence to just happen to meet the real Beauregard Bonner, wouldn't you say?"

"You think she came here looking for him?"

"Or his family. After all, he'd abandoned her and her daughter, right?"

Beau nodded. Carl was right. It would explain the

way she'd looked at him the first night he'd met her. By then, she must have realized the other man had been an imposter. And worse.

"You'll have to tell Rebecca. You don't want her to find out from someone else."

Beau rubbed his hand over his face, his head aching. This was the last thing he'd ever wanted to tell his oldest daughter. There was already bad blood between them. And now this.

"I know how I felt when the old man used to swear I wasn't his son," Carl said thoughtfully. "Was all right by me. I always hoped I wasn't related to the son of a bitch. He used to say he had more bastards around than a female barn cat."

Beau had always heard rumors that Earle Bonner had children all over Texas. He hadn't married Carl's mother, so Beau could definitely understand why Carl would want anyone for a father other than the one he'd had.

Beau cursed their father's soul to hell for the way he'd treated Carl. Beau had tried to make up for it, but all the money in the world couldn't take away the hurt from a father who hadn't wanted his child. Just as Mason had said.

"I would give anything if none of this came to light," Beau said as his brother fell silent. "I tried to convince Dixie not to do this but—"

"She's Dixie and definitely *your* daughter."

Beau lifted his head, hearing something in his brother's voice he'd never heard before. "Do you hold a grudge about the old man's will?"

Carl leaned back in his chair. "I wondered when

you'd get around to that." He laughed and shook his head. "Hell, Beau, I don't know what to do with half the money I have thanks to you. You've been more than generous when the fact is, you didn't have to give me a cent. Our old man is rolling over in his grave right now because of what you've done for me."

Beau didn't know what to say. The old man had always shown favoritism, making it no secret to anyone, especially Carl, that he preferred Beau. But when Earle Bonner had left Beau the farm, he hadn't thought he was doing him a favor. In fact, he'd talked about leaving the farm to Carl, saying Carl deserved to be stuck on the farm the rest of his life. The old man died before the first oil well came in a gusher.

"It was a crappy deal, the way things turned out."

Carl grinned. "Are you kiddin'? Things turned out great. Stop beating yourself up." He rose to his feet. "Just for the record, I didn't know there were any photos hidden in that jewelry box. I retrieved it from where you'd thrown it in the trash because I thought Dixie should have something of her mother's one day."

Beau nodded. "I wasn't thinking clearly back then. I couldn't bear to see anything of hers. You did right."

"I try," Carl said. "Tell Rebecca before she finds out from someone else." He paused. "You don't look good, Beau. You've got to start taking care of yourself." He tapped his fingers over his heart. "Life is short, Beau. Enjoy it a little. Hell, it could all end tomorrow."

Carl left, leaving Beau staring after him. He couldn't help feeling there was still a whole hell of a lot unsaid between them, no matter what Carl professed.

Hadn't he known there were secrets from the past? Secrets that, when they came to light, were going to blow his life to hell.

DIXIE LOOKED OUT at the Montana landscape of towering mountain peaks, snow and endless sky, all her fears coming together in a rush. "What if Glendora was murdered and before she died, she told her killer about Amelia? We have to warn her," she said, digging out her cell phone.

"What are you going to tell her?"

"I don't know. Maybe to go to a neighbor's and stay put until we get there. Or not to answer the door." She reached Information and asked for Amelia McCarthy. No listing. Dixie asked about any other McCarthy's in the Ashton area. Only one. Buzz and Rita McCarthy.

Dixie dialed the number on her cell.

It was answered by a woman on the third ring. She sounded breathless. "Hello?"

"I'm trying to locate an Amelia McCarthy. Amelia Hardaway McCarthy?"

"Yes, she was my sister-in-law," the woman said.

Dixie couldn't help the disappointed sound that escaped her. "She's *deceased?*"

Chance looked away from his driving in surprise.

"Yes, six months ago. Can you tell me what this is about?"

Dixie told her as briefly as possible that her mother had been friends with Amelia and she was hoping to talk to her since her mother had died when she was very young.

"I'm so sorry. What was your mother's name?"

Dixie caught herself before she said Sarah. "Elizabeth Sarah Worth."

"Oh, my gosh. My sister-in-law used to talk about her all the time."

Dixie tried not to get her hopes up. "I don't know much about my mother. I was wondering if Amelia and my mother remained friends after my mother moved to Texas."

"They sure did," Rita McCarthy said. "Your mother wrote my sister-in-law nearly every week. Amelia was so worried about her. Elizabeth was calling herself Sarah and was so unhappy. Then she wrote that she'd found a wonderful man who loved her daughter as his own. She said she had to keep her past a secret, and that bothered her. She really struggled with that. I suppose you know all that, though."

"About the man my mother had two children with before moving to Texas," Dixie said. "Did you ever meet him?"

"No. I wasn't living here then." She seemed to hesitate. "Maybe I shouldn't say this…"

"Please. I'm trying to find out who he was. The man used the name Beauregard Bonner, but that wasn't who he was."

"Oh, my goodness. Well, I can tell you this. My sister-in-law didn't like him. She didn't trust him. He wasn't very nice, I guess."

So Dixie kept hearing. "You said my mother wrote Amelia?"

"That's right. Sarah, that's what she was calling

herself then, was worried that he'd find out that Amelia was writing her so she got a post office box outside Houston. That's how my sister-in-law knew something had happened to her. When a bunch of her unopened letters were returned, she contacted the post office and was told that the box holder hadn't paid her rent for some time and the mail had been returned to the sender."

Dixie felt sick. Her mother had lived a lie all those years.

"It was so wonderful that your mother had finally found happiness. Well, as much as that horrible man would let her. Not her husband, the other man," Rita said. "Amelia told me about how your mother didn't find out that he'd been lying to her until she got to Texas and met the real Beauregard Bonner and was forced to play up to him for money."

Dixie couldn't breathe. She could feel Chance's gaze on her. "What is it?" he whispered.

She shook her head, sucked in a breath and said into the phone, "So it was all about money?"

"Honey, she had no choice. She had her baby girl to take care of and…" Rita seemed to hesitate. "Amelia said that your mother feared for her life if she didn't do what he wanted."

Dixie felt sick. This woman had been her mother. A weak woman who'd fallen for the wrong man, had two children out of wedlock, lied and cheated for money. Was this why her father had no photographs of her? Why he never wanted to talk about her? Because he'd found out the truth?

Dixie didn't know what to say. No wonder her father

hadn't wanted her digging into the past, finding out the truth about her own mother.

She realized that Rita was saying something and tried to focus on the woman's words.

"...the last letter she got from your mother. Sarah wanted to tell your father the truth about her past. She loved him and couldn't go on deceiving him, she said. She said she was going to tell him and asked my sister-in-law to pray for her."

Her mother had fallen for the real Beau Bonner? "Did she tell my father?" Dixie asked.

"Amelia assumed she did. But then the letters stopped and she later found out that your mother had died. I probably shouldn't say this, but Amelia always believed that he killed her."

"My father?" Dixie asked, unable to keep the shock out of her voice.

"No, no, the other one. The one masquerading as Beauregard Bonner. The one who used the past against her to keep getting money out of her."

"Are you saying he *blackmailed* her?"

"He threatened to tell her husband that she'd only married him for his money and once your father knew about her past... It would give a man pause if he knew that she hadn't truly loved him at first. That it had been about the money. What man would believe she'd really fallen in love with him?"

Dixie looked over at Chance. Had her mother told Beauregard the truth about her past? Or had she died before she could? Dixie felt cold inside.

"Amelia finally contacted the newspaper down there and found out about the car accident."

"Her car went into the lake," Dixie said, her voice breaking.

"How horrible for her," Rita said.

Had she also planned to tell the other man? Maybe refused to be blackmailed anymore?

The thought sent a spear of ice down her spine. "Did Amelia keep the letters from my mother? Or any photographs?"

"I'm sorry. Amelia destroyed the letters and all the photos just as Sarah made her promise to do. I think she was afraid for my sister-in-law."

Dixie could understand that. "Is there anything about the man, anything Amelia might have mentioned, that would help me identify him?" The cell phone connection was growing dim as the highway cut through the mountains.

"None I can think of. He was nice-looking enough, I gather. Quite the charmer. But it was so long ago, you know."

Yes, she knew. "Well, thank you. I'm so sorry to hear about Amelia's passing. I wish I could have met her."

"I hope you find what you're looking for, dear."

Dixie glanced over at Chance. She already had.

"AMELIA MCCARTHY IS DEAD," Chance said as Dixie snapped off the phone and leaned back in her seat.

She nodded, devastated. She'd been so sure that Amelia might be able to help them find the man. "I talked to her sister-in-law, Rita McCarthy." She told

him what she'd learned about the letters and what her
mother had planned to do just before her death.

Dixie sighed. "Apparently, my father made her
happy." She had to admit knowing that made her feel a
little better. Maybe they had loved each other. Wasn't
that what every child wanted? For her parents to have
loved each other. Even if it ended badly.

But she couldn't shake the feeling that her mother
had been murdered—and by a man she had once loved.
"He killed her so she couldn't tell my father the truth."

"The police ruled it was an accident, right?"

Dixie rolled her eyes. "Just like Glendora's. My
mother decides to tell my father the truth and ends up
at the bottom of a lake. Don't tell me the timing doesn't
make you suspicious."

"Everything makes me suspicious. What if it does
turn out that he's a killer, that he not only killed your
mother, but is the one who hired the men to come after
you? He's Rebecca's *father*."

His words chilled her. She was looking for a man
who was contemptuous, probably capable of anything.
She hadn't focused on the fact that this man, whoever
he was, was Rebecca's father.

Dixie shook her head, fighting emotions she wasn't
used to. Normally she was in control. But she'd set
something in motion and there seemed to be no stopping
it. She wished she'd never begun digging into the past.

"Can you imagine how this will hurt Rebecca?"
Chance said. "This will devastate her."

She nodded, fighting tears, as he reached over to
squeeze her hand. "There's no reason to go to Idaho."

"No."

"What do we do, Chance?"

"We meet your father's plane tomorrow. We tell him what we know. Maybe with the information you've gathered and his help, we can figure out what the hell is going on."

She studied his handsome face. "You think my father knows the man, don't you?"

"I think it's a real possibility," he said as the land stretched ahead of them in rolling wheat fields. "Otherwise, why was your mother so afraid to tell him the truth? She saw that other man as a threat. I think he stayed around to get money, to make sure she never told."

"This man has gotten away with it all these years," Dixie said, aching at the thought of what her mother had gone through. "Who could he be?"

"That's the million-dollar question, isn't it?"

"Million and a *half*," Dixie said, remembering what Chance had told her about the ransom demand. "He tried to make it look like a kidnapping to cover up the real reason I was going to be killed."

She felt Chance look over at her, then back at his driving. "Looks that way." She watched him glance into her rearview mirror, saw his expression.

She turned, afraid of what she would see. Her fear ratcheted up another notch as she saw a van that looked exactly like the one she'd seen in the parking garage the night this had all begun.

Chapter Fourteen

Chance had expected trouble once they left the interstate and got on the two-lane Highway 287 headed north toward Townsend. There had been enough traffic that he hadn't been able to spot a tail, but he now suspected they'd been followed since Livingston.

Traffic was horrendous around Bozeman, but once they left there and drove west, it began to thin out.

Most of the cars had ski racks on top. Some out-of-state plates, people up here for the Christmas vacation. With Big Sky Ski Resort only forty miles to the south and Bridger Bowl about twenty to the north, Bozeman had become a winter destination along with being the home of Montana State University and ten-thousand-plus college students.

Chance swore under his breath as the van closed the distance between them, but didn't even attempt to pass even when he slowed down.

The road narrowed along the Missouri River, dropping away on each side. There was no guardrail on either side and little traffic. This was the stretch of highway where the van driver would make his move.

Chance sped up. The van sped up, as well, keeping the same distance between them. The road curved as it wound by the slow-moving, dark, ice-rimmed river.

The van closed some of the distance between them.

"That's the two men who attacked me in the parking garage," Dixie said, looking back.

He heard the tremor in her voice. "Put the dog on the floor," he ordered. "And brace yourself."

They were almost to the bridge. The van filled the rearview mirror just an instant before the bumper slammed into the back of the pickup.

Chance swore as he fought to keep the truck under control. Out of the corner of his eye, he saw Dixie's face. It was leeched of all color, her blue eyes wide with fear. He met her eyes and saw something flicker in her gaze.

"Give me your gun," she said, her voice breaking.

"What?"

The van slammed into the back of them again. The pickup fishtailed, one tire going off the edge of the road and kicking up snow that blew over the van's windshield, forcing the driver to hit his wipers and back off a little.

Dixie unhooked her seat belt and got on her knees to face the back window. The pickup was made for a camper in the bed so it had a small sliding window that she now unlatched. Cold air rushed in.

"Get back in your seat!" Chance yelled as the van came at them again. He sped up, but ahead was another tight curve, the drop-off much steeper on each side of the road.

"Give me your gun," she said over the roar of the van's engine as it came at them again.

The van slammed into the bumper. Chance gripped

the wheel, fighting to keep the truck on the road as Dixie held on to the back of the seat with one hand and reached under his coat, unsnapped the holster and withdrew the gun.

"You don't even know how to shoot a gun," he said, swearing as he heard her snap off the safety.

"Slow down," she said, sounding almost too calm.

He shot her a look. She was braced on the back of the seat, the weapon gripped in both hands and pointing out through the small window opening, the cold wind whipping her hair, her eyes narrowed in concentration.

A sharp turn was just ahead with steep drop-offs on each side of the pavement. The van driver started to make another run at them.

"Hang on," Chance said, and hit his brakes.

The move took the driver of the van by surprise. In his rearview mirror, Chance saw the driver literally stand on his brakes. The van fishtailed wildly just before it struck the back of the pickup with a force that sent the pickup rocketing forward.

The shot was deafening as it echoed through the cab of the pickup. Chance managed to just barely keep the truck on the pavement, the right back tire dropping dangerously over the edge of the highway before he got it back.

In his side-view mirror he saw the van's windshield shatter into a web of white an instant before it blew out, showering the driver and the man next to him with tiny cubes of glass. The driver of the van was also fighting to regain control of his vehicle.

Chance swore as he saw the passenger level his own weapon at the pickup. At Dixie. "Get down!" he yelled.

Dixie got off another shot that boomed in the cab. In that same instant, Chance saw the front tire blow on the van, saw the driver fight to get the vehicle under control. It was the next sound that took his breath away.

A shot fired from the van. It thundered just behind him, metal chips flying from where it had struck the cab and ricocheted.

Dixie fell over in the seat as Chance took the curve.

"Dixie!" He reached for her, glancing in the rearview mirror as his hand found her shoulder, fear spiking. "Dixie!"

"I'm all right," Dixie said in a small voice.

"Are you hit?"

"I'm all right."

He stole a look at her and saw the tiny cuts from the flying metal on her face oozing blood, and swore.

Behind him he watched as the van driver lost control, the blown tire flapping and throwing up chunks of debris. The van skidded sideways, the blown tire rim digging into the asphalt. The van rolled twice before it left the highway and tumbled down the embankment and disappeared.

Chance hit the brakes, coming to a stop at the edge of the road. He was shaking as he looked over at Dixie. Tears welled in her eyes and she chewed at her lower lip.

"Who taught you to shoot?" he said.

"I'm from Texas," she said. "Do you think they're—"

The explosion drowned out her words as behind them the sky filled with a ball of fire.

Chance did a highway patrol turn and drove back toward the smoke and flames, pulling to a stop at the edge of the highway. The van was consumed in flames. In stunned silence they watched it burn, clouds of smoke billowing up into the winter evening.

There were no footprints in the snow around the van. No bodies. The men hadn't gotten out.

Dixie stared at the smoke pouring up from the van, shaking so hard her teeth chattered. She fought tears as she stared at the van, imagining the charred remains of the men inside.

"Are you all right?" Chance asked as he took the gun from her hands and closed the back window.

She nodded, telling herself that they would have killed her and Chance, remembering the one who'd kicked her in the head, reliving the night in the parking garage in Houston. But it did little to take away the appalling shock that she'd killed two men just as certainly as if she'd shot them to death.

"I know how you feel right now, if that helps."

She looked over at him and nodded. It did help. She didn't know what she would have done if he hadn't been with her.

"You saved our lives," he said softly, and brushed his fingers over her cheek.

She nodded, tears blurring her eyes as he dragged her into his arms. Behind them several cars had pulled up. One of the drivers jumped out and ran up to the side of the pickup.

Dixie pulled back from Chance's embrace as the man tapped on the window.

"Have you already called in the accident?" the man asked, looking from Dixie's tearful face to Chance's.

"Our cell phone isn't working," Chance said. "Can you call it in?"

"Any survivors?" the man asked.

Dixie watched Chance shake his head. "Saw it happen in the rearview mirror."

"Looks like the driver lost control and missed the curve," the man said. "I'll call it in."

"Thanks," Chance said, and waited until the man got back into his vehicle to place the call before he shifted the pickup into first and pulled away. Up the road he turned around and headed north again.

Dixie felt numb, everything surreal. She wanted to believe it was over. The men who'd tried to kill her were dead. But whoever had hired them wasn't.

Beauregard jumped up on the seat next to her again. She wrapped her arms around the dog's neck as she buried her face in his soft fur. This was far from over.

BEAU PICKED UP THE PHONE and held it for a long moment as he thought about how he was going to tell Rebecca.

Hell, he had no idea. How did you tell a woman like Rebecca that her whole life had been a lie?

He put down the phone, then picked it up again and hurriedly dialed Rebecca's number before he lost his nerve.

Rebecca answered after four rings. He could hear soft music in the background, the soft clink of expensive crystal, hushed voices. A party?

"Rebecca?"

Silence.

"Is this about Dixie?"

"No. I need to see you."

"What's happened?" She sounded scared.

"Honey, where are you? Could I come over?"

"What? Tonight? Now? Can't it wait?"

"No. Rebecca. There's something I should have told you a long time ago. Now that Dixie's... Well, there's just things about your mother that..." He stopped himself. "Anyway, I don't want to do this on the phone."

"Something Dixie told you?" Rebecca said. "Daddy, I have company. I'm sure whatever it is can wait until morning. Why don't I come over to your house in the morning first thing? I hope you don't take anything Dixie says too seriously. You know how she is."

"Yes." He wished that were the case this time. Beau hated the relief he felt. "In the morning then." And yet he didn't want to break the connection. "Rebecca, I love you." He waited and realized after a moment that she'd already hung up.

BY THE TIME Chance reached Townsend, it had begun to snow. He drove through town as snowflakes spiraled down. At a stop sign, he watched a young couple pick through the last of the Christmas trees in an empty lot. The falling snow blurred the red-and-green strands of lights strung around the lot. There was something hypnotizing about watching the snowflakes drift down through the lights.

"Where are we going?" Dixie asked dully.

"Home." It was Christmas Eve and the only place he wanted to be was the cabin. He felt a need to go home. He wanted to believe that the death of the two hit men in the van would be the end of it. But whoever had hired them was still alive and if he knew anything about secrets and the people who tried to keep them, that person wouldn't let it end here. But that was another reason he wanted to go home. Let it end on his turf rather than along some lonesome two-lane.

As he drove down the main drag, he heard a Christmas carol being piped out from one of the bars. He looked over at Dixie. She appeared shell-shocked. From the night she was attacked in the parking garage, she'd been running on adrenaline and bravado, but clearly she'd run out of both.

He knew she hadn't had time to assimilate everything, let alone the impact of what had happened and what she'd learned. She needed some down time.

"I'm taking you to my cabin."

She looked over at him, her gaze softening as she nodded, her smile small. She'd been through so much.

He pulled into a gas station with a convenience store and filled up while she went inside. He found her sitting in a small plastic booth, her hands wrapped around a foam cup of hot coffee, her eyes hollow.

He got himself a cup of coffee. They still had a long drive out to the lake and he had no idea what they would find. For all he knew there might be someone out there waiting for them.

"Have you talked to my father?" she asked.

His eyes locked with hers. "No."

She nodded and put down her cup. Not even caffeine could keep her system revved up anymore. "I'm so tired," she said in a voice he'd never heard before. She met his gaze, hers filling with tears. "I'm tired of running. Tired of being scared. I'm just…tired."

He nodded, smiling his sympathy as he reached across the table and touched her fingers. They were ice-cold. "It's going to be over soon." That he did believe. The outcome he couldn't promise, though. "I will protect you to my last dying breath."

She smiled, a tired teary smile. "I knew you would."

"Come on, Dix," he said, rising to pull her to her feet. He scooped up the box of groceries he'd bought and, with his free arm around her, walked her to the pickup. She cuddled next to Beauregard and was asleep before Chance even had the engine started.

As Chance turned onto the road into the cabin, he stopped to study the tracks. The new snow had filled the only tracks in or out—his tracks from over thirty-six hours before.

No one else had been down the road. He shifted into four-wheel drive, the pickup bucking the deep snow, headlights bobbing through snowcapped pines. The only sound was the roar of the engine as he drove, his headlights finally flashing on the cabin ahead, filling him with such a sense of relief that it made him weak.

He pulled up beside the house. Beauregard lifted his head and began to wag his tail. Chance wasn't the only one glad to finally be home.

He opened his door and Beauregard bounded over the top of him and out into the snow.

Dixie had awakened and was looking out through the snowy darkness at the cabin. Some of her color had returned and she looked less beaten down. It buoyed his spirits to see her strength.

"Home," he said, feeling almost shy.

"You built it," she said.

He nodded, studying her. In some ways, she was so like her father. Stubborn. Self-confident. Determined. And at the top of the list: inquisitive to a fault.

"Is there anything you don't know about me?" he asked, only half joking.

She turned then to look at him. The falling snow cast a silky light into the cab of the pickup. "No, I don't think so. But if there is time, I wouldn't mind learning more."

He laughed. "Nice to have you back, Dixie," he said, and got out.

As Dixie stepped into the cabin, he tried to see his home through her eyes. He'd always been proud of the place since he'd built it himself. But now it seemed too functional. It lacked warmth, what some might have called a woman's touch. Strange that he'd never noticed that before.

"It's not much, but it's home," he said.

She said nothing as she seemed to take it all in. Finally she turned to look at him. "It's wonderful. I love it." She smiled and her smile alone warmed the whole place and made it seem better instantly.

He smiled his thanks and let out the breath he hadn't realized he'd been holding. "I'll get a fire going. You must be freezing." As he made the fire, he watched her out of the corner of his eye. She moved through the place touching the stones he'd laid, running her fingers along the logs he'd peeled by hand, stopping to study a photograph he'd taken of the lake one summer evening at sunset.

That life seemed a million years ago now. He felt as

if he could barely remember it. That's what only a couple of days with Dixie Bonner did to a man. When she left, the cabin would seem vacuous and empty. He found himself dreading that inevitable day.

As he got the logs crackling in the firebox, she came to stand next to it, her eyes shiny as she looked into the flames. He knew she was thinking about the two men who'd lost their lives today. He knew what it was like to take another life. To look into a person's eyes that instant before he pulled the trigger and saw them die.

He hoped never to have to pull that trigger again. But unless he quit the P.I. business and took up a job as a ranch hand again....

"What is today?" Dixie asked.

"Christmas Eve."

She nodded and held her hands out to the fire.

He glanced past her at the cabin. There was no sign anywhere that it was Christmas. Not that he would have decorated even if he hadn't taken this latest job. He didn't do Christmas. Hadn't since his daughter's last one three years ago.

"Hungry?" he asked.

To his surprise, Dixie shook her head.

In the kitchen, he put away the groceries and saw that Dixie had moved to the front window.

Through the falling snow, the lake appeared endless. Nothing but white into the darkness. The snow blanketed the cabin and lake in cold silence.

"Can I help?" she asked, as if sensing him watching her.

"You cook?" He hadn't meant to sound so skeptical.

She cocked her head at him, a warning look in her eye.

He raised his hands in surrender and laughed. "Go ahead, tell me you're a gourmet cook, you've won prizes and that I'm the worst chauvinist you've ever met."

She shook her head, started to say something, but seemed to lose the words. She turned away but not before he'd seen her face crumple.

He dropped the groceries on the counter and rushed to her. "Dixie?" He put his hands on her shoulders and turned her to him. She was crying, huge shuddering sobs. He thumbed away her tears, cupping her face in both hands. "Dixie." Her name was a whisper on his lips as he pulled her into his arms. "Oh, Dixie."

He let her cry as he held her and stroked her hair, her back, all the time trying to soothe her with soft words and gentle caresses.

The sobs subsided, her trembling body stilled, softening as it fit to his. She felt so right in his arms. He had the thought that he never wanted to let her go.

He pulled back, realizing the foolishness of that. Her lower lip trembled as she looked up at him.

He bent toward her as if he didn't have a mind of his own. His lips brushed over hers, her mouth sweet and supple with just the hint of salty tears.

He knew he should stop, but her lips parted as he deepened the kiss, opening to him as her body melded again into his.

He breathed her in, all his senses acutely in tune with her. Desire rippled through him in waves each stronger than the next. He'd never wanted anyone the way he wanted this woman. This damned woman had more than gotten to him.

To his surprise it was Dixie who pulled back this time. The look in her eyes surprised him. He'd thought this was what she'd wanted.

"What?" he asked, half-afraid.

"I have to know something first."

"I'm sorry, I thought…"

"That I wanted you?" She smiled up at him. "Oh, I do, Chance. I *always* have."

He caught his breath as he sensed exactly where this was going.

"But I have to know if it's me you're kissing. Or my sister."

"Rebecca? Dixie, she's married with three kids."

"You were in love with her."

"A lifetime ago. Dixie, that kiss was about you. No one else." He reached for her. "Oh, Dixie," he said as he brushed a lock of her wild hair back from her beautiful face. "There is no one like you. No one who's ever made me feel like this."

She looked into Chance Walker's eyes and saw the answer she needed, had wanted since the first day she'd set eyes on him when she was twelve. It had been love at first sight, as corny as that was. No schoolgirl crush. She'd known that someday—

"Dixie, you have to know that I..." She dragged him to her, cutting off his words with a kiss. He swept her up in his arms, kissing her wildly, as he carried her to the deep leather couch in front of the fire.

He made love to her slowly in the firelight, kissing her as he removed each piece of clothing before he began a seductive trail of kisses across her bare flesh.

She arched against his mouth as he pushed aside her bra to suck one of her hard nipples into his mouth. Unlike him, she tore at his clothes, yearning to feel his naked body on hers.

"Dixie," he whispered as she tossed his shirt over the back of the couch. "We have all night."

She laughed, breathing hard as she reached for the buttons on his jeans, arching one brow as she met his gaze. "Then let's not waste a second of it," she said, and jerked his jeans open.

They rolled off the couch onto the braided rug in front of the fire, both laughing as they shed the rest of their clothing.

She pressed her naked flesh to his, taking in his scent, burying her fingers in his thick hair as she looked into his eyes. "Now," she said, "we can slow down." She met his mouth with her own, felt his hands cup her breasts, his thumbs teasing the nipples to hard, pleasured points before his fingers slid down her belly and between her legs.

He laughed and rolled her over onto her back. She arched against his fingers, then his mouth before she cried out in release. Then his body was back, warm and hard, as he fitted himself into her and began the slow sweet dance of lovers until they both cried out, clutching each other as the fire crackled softly beside them, the snow falling silently beyond the windows.

For a long time they lay in each others arms watching the fire, dazed and drowsy. Dixie couldn't remember being more content. That was one reason she was so surprised when she felt Chance pull away to get to his feet.

"Stay here," he ordered, then leaned over her and kissed her gently on the mouth before he dressed and went to the door. "I'll be right back."

WARMED BY THEIR lovemaking, she lay in front of the fire until she realized she was ravenous. She dressed and went into the kitchen to make them sandwiches. When Chance didn't come back, she began to worry. She missed him, and that reminded her that this was temporary. Maybe very temporary given that someone still wanted her dead. And now she'd involved Chance in it.

She was just finishing putting the sandwich makings away when she heard his footfalls on the deck. The next moment, the front door burst open and she caught the rich scent of pine as a huge pine tree was pushed through the door followed by a snowy Chance Walker.

He was smiling as he stood the tree up in a pot by the window. "I have no idea what we're going to decorate it with," he said, eyes shining when he looked at her. "I got rid of all my decorations."

She nodded, pretty sure she knew when that had happened and why. "Don't worry. We'll find something." She touched the prickly green bough, tears filling her eyes as she looked at him. "Thank you."

"It's Christmas," he said, his voice cracking.

CHANCE KNEW that no matter what happened in the future, he would never forget this night. *This* Christmas. Like the last one with his daughter, he would keep it always in his heart.

They made a huge batch of popcorn, eating some in

front of the fire, stringing the rest on thread. They talked about religion and flying saucers and Bigfoot. They laughed and kidded. They kissed. And by midnight, the tree was decorated.

As they stood back and admired it, he had to admit, "I've never seen a more beautiful tree."

Dixie laughed. He loved the sound. It filled the cabin the same way her smile did, bringing a warmth that filled him to overflowing. He never thought he could feel like this again.

"I want to tell you about my daughter," he said after a moment. She nodded slowly. And he told her about a woman he'd been dating. "When she got pregnant I offered to marry her, but we both knew it wouldn't have worked. She moved in here, had the baby on Christmas Eve three years ago. I never thought I could be happier."

Dixie put her arm around him, knowing what came next.

"Her name was Star. She lived for just over three weeks. Her heart hadn't formed correctly." He fought back tears. "She was so beautiful."

Dixie took him in her arms. He buried his face in her hair. They stayed like that for a long time. When he pulled back he saw that she was crying. He thumbed away her tears.

"You know what our tree needs, don't you?" Dixie said, getting up to go to the kitchen.

He smiled, nodding as he saw what she planned to do.

He cut a star from the cardboard box their groceries had been in and she covered it with tin foil.

"Here," she said. "You can put it on the tree."

He shook his head and grabbed her, swinging her around as he carried her over to the tree to lift her up as she placed the star carefully on the top. The firelight caught it, sending the silvery light across the log walls of the cabin.

"Merry Christmas!" she said as he lowered her to the floor again.

He felt a well of emotion surge inside him as he pulled her to him. "Merry Christmas," he whispered against her hair, and kissed her.

Sometime during the wee hours of morning they fell asleep in each other's arms, Beauregard snoring softly in the corner as the fire burned down to embers and the snow continued to fall.

Chapter Fifteen

Oliver stumbled into the house, half-drunk, sick to his very soul. He thought about sleeping on the couch, not wanting to wake Rebecca, but at the same time not wanting to have to face the rowdy kids in the morning.

Then he saw a note saying that the nanny had taken the kids somewhere. It was just him and Rebecca alone here tonight. The thought sent a shiver through him. Had she purposely sent the nanny and the brats away? Was she upstairs lying in wait for him because she knew?

The thought made him sick to his stomach.

He headed for the couch, planning to avoid her as long as possible. The phone rang.

He hurriedly snatched it up before it could wake her. Who could be calling at this hour anyway? "Hello?"

"Bad news."

Oliver's head buzzed as his heart pounded. "Ace?"

"The deal fell through. The money's gone. I've been trying to track the guys down all day. They blew town. I'm sorry."

"No." Oliver was shaking his head, thinking about

how that money was going to save him. He was ruined. Worse than ruined. Even his name would be dragged through the mud. He'd be lucky to get out with the clothes on his back once Beau found out. "No."

"I'm sorry, man. You knew there was risk, right? I mean, you can't expect to make millions with a few measly thousand dollars without there being risks."

"Two hundred and twenty-five thousand," Oliver said. "This can't be happening."

"I know what you mean, man. I put some of my money into this. That's why I'm leaving town for a while."

"What?"

"I owe the kind of guys who break your kneecaps just for the fun of it. You're lucky you don't owe any guys like that anyway."

Was he kidding? He owed everyone. And he'd lost more tonight. He was as good as dead. "You can't leave town. We have to find these guys and get the money back."

"Not happening. I'm out of here and I doubt I'll be coming back anytime soon. You might want to think about leaving town for a while." The line went dead.

"Ace? Ace!" He slammed down the phone, the sound echoing through the foyer. He leaned against the wall. He was totally screwed. There was no way out now. Nothing he could do.

He thought about the gun he kept in the nightstand beside his bed in case of a break-in. There was only one way out, he thought in his drunken, desolate state. Go up there, put the gun to his head and pull the trigger.

And if he wanted to be really considerate, he would take Rebecca with him. After all, this was all her fault.

The thought buoyed him enough that he slowly pushed himself off the wall and began the long climb up the stairs to the master bedroom.

DIXIE WOKE sometime in the night. She'd heard a sound outside the cabin. She closed her eyes, not wanting to get up. The cabin felt cold and here in bed with Chance, she couldn't have been more warm and content.

Beauregard let out a soft woof in the other room. Chance didn't stir. She smiled to herself, remembering their hours of lovemaking. Any other man would have been comatose.

Slipping out of the bed, she padded into the living room. The fire was little more than ashes, the room cold, at least by Texas standards.

She hugged herself as she moved to the window where Beauregard was staring out. He let out another woof, glancing over at her as if to say, "There's something out there."

"Right," she said, thinking it was probably a deer. Chance said there were often deer in his yard.

She put her face to the glass, cupping her hands to look out. It was still snowing, the sky light for the middle of the night. But still she couldn't see anything. If there was a deer out there, she sure didn't see it.

She started to turn away when she thought she saw a light. It flashed on for a few seconds off to her right, low on the mountain, and then was gone just as quickly. She stared into the snowy darkness until her eyes ached but she didn't see it again.

Even Beauregard lost interest. He dropped down to

go back over to his spot next to the fireplace. She stayed a few more minutes, becoming convinced she'd just imagined it. Who in their right mind would be out on a night like this? And didn't Chance say there were no other cabins close by?

She got herself a glass of water, checked the door to make sure it was locked and went back to bed.

"Everything all right?" Chance asked sleepily as she crawled under the covers.

"Fine." Locked in the warmth of Chance's arms, everything *was* fine.

OLIVER CREPT INTO the master bedroom afraid to turn on a light. What he had to do was better done in the dark. He'd cried all the way up the stairs, stopping on the landing to sit.

He'd never felt more sorry for himself. He tried to imagine his parents at the funeral mourning over his grave. They would be sorry they'd treated him the way they had all of his life. Cold, uncaring snobs, that's what they were.

The bedroom was pitch-black—just the way Rebecca liked it. He silently cursed her as he stumbled in the general direction of the bedstand where he kept the gun, all the time imagining his parents breaking down at the funeral. They would be so sorry.

They'd never wanted him to marry Rebecca. They found her to be inferior in class. *But she's rich,* he'd said. They'd turned their noses up at Beauregard Bonner's new wealth as being crass just like him.

He hoped they'd feel guilty for the rest of their lives.

In fact, he might write a suicide note telling them they were the reason. Why not?

He bumped into the bed and froze, afraid he'd awaken Rebecca. Not a sound came from the bed. He worked his way along the edge to the bedstand, opened the drawer and pulled out the gun.

Rebecca always slept on the left side.

He couldn't see her, but then he didn't really want to. Better just to get it done quickly.

He clicked off the safety, crying again. Not at the thought of shooting Rebecca, but at pulling the trigger on himself. He told himself this would save Rebecca the embarrassment of the divorce. She would thank him if she knew what he was doing for her. It wasn't like she would forgive him once she found out about the money. The cold-hearted bitch.

With his legs against the bed, he estimated the distance from where he stood to where Rebecca's head would be on her pillow. Aiming the gun, he braced himself. Two shots for her. One for him. Drunk and desperate, he decided he didn't have the energy to write a suicide note. Let his parents always wonder.

He closed his eyes and pulled the trigger. Boom. Boom. He opened one eye. He couldn't see Rebecca in the bed but there was no sound coming from her.

Knowing there was no turning back now, he turned the gun on himself.

BEAU BONNER GOT THE CALL early the next morning. At first he didn't recognize the voice. He had trouble making sense of the words the man was saying.

"What the hell are you talking about?" he finally demanded when he realized it was one of his pilots.

"Your jet, sir. It's gone."

"What do you mean, gone? Stolen?" Beau remembered that Mason had taken it. This was just a misunderstanding. "Mason Roberts took it—"

"No, sir. I'm talking about the jet you instructed me to fly to Montana today," the pilot said. "It was taken last night and I'm told it won't be back for several days."

Beau felt his blood pressure soar. "Who took it? Carl? That damned irresponsible cousin of his, Ace?"

"Apparently you gave your daughter Rebecca Lancaster permission to take it. She hired her own pilot."

"What?" He couldn't believe this. "Where the hell did she go with it?"

"According to her flight plan? New York City and possibly on to Paris."

Beau snapped off the phone, so livid he thought he might have a coronary. What the hell had Rebecca been thinking?

He groaned as he realized exactly what she'd been thinking. She didn't want to hear what he had to tell her. That was so like Rebecca. She'd never wanted to hear bad news. She preferred to pretend that everything was fine.

Beau cussed to himself. He should have gone to her house, made her listen. Well, at least in New York she wouldn't hear about what was going on in Montana. There would be time when she returned to tell her everything.

He felt as if he'd dodged the bullet yet another time

and felt guilty for being relieved he wouldn't have to face Rebecca this morning. Christmas morning.

What now? He'd have to call Chance to tell him he wouldn't be sending a plane. With commercial flights booked solid this time of year, Beau knew there was little chance of getting Dixie back to Texas for Christmas now. Christmas, and he was all alone.

He had hoped they could all be together this Christmas like normal families. Were there normal families? He blamed himself for Dixie and Rebecca never getting along. He loved Rebecca with all his heart, but it had never seemed enough. Even as a child, she'd seemed incapable of being satisfied. He'd poured love into her, trying to make up for the father who hadn't wanted her. But Rebecca had proved to be a bottomless pit.

And then Dixie had come along.

Just the opposite of Rebecca, Dixie had been a willful, independent child who didn't seem to need anyone. He'd blamed that on her having to grow up without a mother from such a young age. But the truth was, Dixie was like him.

Beau had spent his life trying not to be like his father and yet he could see the similarities between Rebecca and Dixie, him and Carl. Carl had wanted their father's love desperately. Beau hadn't asked for it, knew he didn't deserve that kind of high regard, and often despised their mean domineering father as much as Carl.

Beau hadn't stayed on the farm out of love or loyalty. While everyone his age left to find good-paying jobs and adventure, Beau had stayed on the farm in Texas, knowing there wasn't any other place he'd be special except in his father's eyes.

And then a gusher came in a few farms away and his friends came back to work the rigs. Carl and Ace had returned to Texas along with Mason who'd been bumming around the country. Mason came to him, not just with stories of the places he'd been, but with an idea.

To scrape together all the money they had and have a test well dug on the isolated north forty of the farm so no one would get wind of it—especially Carl or Ace. Or Beau's old man.

He put his head in his hands. Rebecca had always believed that he loved Dixie more. Once she heard he wasn't her father, nothing would convince her otherwise.

The phone rang again. This time it was the police.

CHANCE CAME AWAKE slowly, fighting not to leave the warm contentment of the dream. He'd been so happy in the dream, happier than he could remember being.

He opened his eyes to find sunlight streaming into the cabin. For those first few seconds he thought he was alone—just as he'd been for so long.

Then he felt her beside him and closed his eyes tight to hold back the sudden rush of emotion. It hadn't been a dream. Beside him, Dixie stirred, her naked body warm and luscious next to his.

Opening his eyes, he looked at her, shocked by his feelings of just seeing her beside him, let alone the memory of their lovemaking. At that moment he would have moved heaven and earth to keep her beside him.

That thought made him carefully slide out of the bed and leave the bedroom. He found his clothing and dressed before building a fire and jotting Dixie a note. Beauregard bound up the moment the dog saw that they would be going outside. The snow was deep but Chance didn't take the time to shovel, Beauregard busting a trail ahead of him through a world of cold white.

He thought about taking the pickup, but decided to hike down the road until he could get cell phone service. The land lay in frozen silence. He stood in the deep snow, breathing in the scent of pine. He needed this time alone on this beautiful Christmas morning.

Bonner answered on the first ring. "Rebecca?"

"No," Chance said, frowning. "It's Chance."

"I thought it would be Rebecca." He sounded half-asleep. Or half-drunk. "She took my plane to New York or Paris. I don't know."

"The plane you were bringing to Montana today," Chance guessed, and swore under his breath.

"Mason has the other one. I don't know when either of them will be back. I'm trying to line up another plane."

"Beau, listen, this can't wait. Dixie and I found out some things about the man your wife had an affair with before she met you that I think you need to know. If you don't already."

Now it was Bonner's turn to swear. "I told you I don't know anything about him and I don't want to."

"You don't have a choice. I'm pretty sure he's the person who hired the two men who were trying to kill Dixie before she could unearth his identity."

"Are you sure this isn't just another of Dixie's—"

"Two men tried to run us off the road yesterday," Chance snapped. "The same two men Dixie says abducted her and ransacked her house looking for her research on her mother's family. The men are dead, but whoever hired them is still out there."

"Oh, my God," Bonner said. "Then it's true. Someone really is trying to kill her?"

"What the hell do you think I've been trying to tell you? And Dixie's aunt is dead, as well."

"My God. I was so sure—"

Chance tried to understand how Bonner must feel right now. Given the other tricks Dixie had played on Bonner, Chance could understand why he hadn't believe it. Mostly Bonner hadn't wanted to believe it. He'd have to share some of the blame if it were true since he hadn't been honest with Dixie when she'd come to him with the photographs.

"You think it's the man Sarah was involved with before me," Bonner said. "You have any idea who he is?"

"No, but from what we found out, he's someone who knows you. He used your name while he was living up here. Your wife's name was actually Elizabeth Sarah Worth. She changed it to Sarah when this man took her to Texas. By then, oil had been found on your farm." Chance hesitated.

"No," Bonner said, as if suspecting where Chance was headed with this.

"She changed her name to Sarah and went after you and your money."

"I don't believe it." But the tremor in his voice said he did.

"The man blackmailed her into doing it," Chance said. "It seems Sarah had a good friend in Idaho who she wrote to every week." He heard Bonner make a small, sad sound. "I assume you didn't know about Amelia McCarthy?"

"No." His voice was muffled.

Chance hated that he had to tell Bonner this over the phone. But the sooner Bonner had the information, the sooner maybe they could find the killer.

"In the last letter that Sarah sent, she said she'd fallen in love with you. She was happy. She said she could no longer live with the lies of her past and planned to tell you the truth."

Bonner sounded as if he was crying. "She never told me."

"The man had been blackmailing her, threatening to tell you. She was giving him money to keep him quiet. Apparently she was also afraid of him."

There was a painful choking sound on the other end of the line. "If you tell me that he—"

"Sarah's friend believed that the man killed her to keep you from learning the truth," Chance finished.

"My God," Bonner said.

"I'm telling you this because I think this man believes that once Dixie is stopped, the truth will never come out. He still has something to lose if you find out who he is. Do you have any idea who he might be?" Silence. "Bonner?"

Chance swore. Beauregard Bonner had hung up. He tried him back, but the line was busy. He tried again, walking farther up the road. This time it rang and rang.

Just as Chance was going to hang up and try again, thinking he must have dialed wrong, he saw the footprints in the snow.

DIXIE WOKE to a chill in the air. She felt in the bed for Chance only to find him gone. She knew he wouldn't have gone far, but still it filled her with a sense of loss. She didn't want to waste a second because eventually this would be over and they would go their separate ways. If they lived that long.

Hadn't she warned herself not to hope for more than what Chance could give her? She knew he'd been hurt badly in the past. It was no coincidence that his relationships were few and far between and little more than a few dates.

He liked living out here alone. He needed it. She understood the choice between living alone or being with the wrong person. Roy Bob Jackson had tempted her, made her realize that she wanted someone in her life. But it had never been Roy Bob Jackson—even if she hadn't found out he worked for her father.

No, it had always been Chance Walker.

She smiled as she remembered their lovemaking, regretting nothing. If this was all they ever shared, then she could live with that. At least, she hoped she could.

Rising, she tiptoed across the cold wood floor to open the bedroom door. Chance had a blaze going in the fireplace. She sniffed the air, hoping for the smell of bacon frying. And French toast, she thought. She always ate hers with brown sugar, honey and butter and had gotten Chance to try it years ago in Texas when she was just a silly kid with a crush.

She wondered if he still ate his French toast that way as she went through the living room picking up her clothing and putting it on as she moved.

But Chance wasn't in the kitchen. Instead she found a note stuck to the coffeemaker.

"Gone up the road to make a cell phone call. Be right back."

Did that mean there wasn't cell phone service in the cabin? She started the coffee and while it brewed, she found her purse and tried *her* cell phone which she'd turned off after talking to Amelia's sister-in-law, Rita McCarthy. The service was unreliable, but she did have a message. She played the message, surprised to hear Rita McCarthy's voice.

"After I talked to you, I got to thinking," Rita said. "I remembered something. Give me a call."

Rita had remembered something. About the man? Dixie went to the window and looked out, hoping to see Chance returning. But there was only his tracks and the dog's in the deep snow of the deck.

She moved to the bedroom window at the back of the cabin and peered out. She could see where he and the dog had walked up the road.

A thud toward the front of the house startled her. Maybe Chance and Beauregard had taken a different way back. Padding into the living room, she glanced out the front window again. No sign of anyone.

She jumped as a large clump of snow came sliding off the metal roof of the cabin to land in a pile just off the deck. Her heart was racing and for a moment, she reconsidered hiking up the road to find Chance. But what if he took another way back and she missed him?

It wasn't as if she'd get lost. All she had to do was to follow the road back. On impulse, she scribbled her note on the bottom of Chance's, that way he'd know where to find her if she did miss him. She was too impatient to wait for him to return. She had to know what Rita had remembered.

Tucking her cell phone into her pocket, she looked around for her coat and boots. Another thud outside. She glanced toward the window as she pulled on her boots and slipped into her coat.

As she opened the door, she felt the wind and heard the groan of the pines. Snow fell from a pine near the edge of the deck, startling her. Why was she nervous?

Because she had a feeling that in a few minutes she would know the identity of the man who wanted her dead.

CHANCE BENT OVER the tracks in the snow. Footprints. Snow had partially filled the tracks, making it hard for him to gauge the size of the boots that had made the prints.

It appeared someone had walked up the snow-filled road, then dropped down the side of the mountain.

He glanced back into the direction of his cabin, a good mile back and down another even less-traveled road flanked on each side by pines.

The tracks in the snow could be from someone going to one of the nearer cabins along the lake. Someone checking to make sure his cabin hadn't been broken into. This time of year all but his cabin was boarded up for winter.

"What do you think, old boy?" Chance said to Beauregard.

The dog's head came up at the sound of Chance's voice. There was snow on the mutt's nose from where he'd been sniffing the tracks.

"Yeah, that's what I was thinking," Chance said.

Heart in his throat, he dropped off the road, following the tracks in the new snow as quickly as he could along the steep frozen bank to the edge of the lake.

The snow was deep, the going slow. He had to wonder why anyone would have come this way. Why not stay on the road where the walking was easier?

He passed one cabin after another, following the tracks to where they picked up a second set. He stopped, surprised to see that these were older, possibly from last night during the storm.

The new footprints began to follow the older set.

Chance frowned. Beauregard was frolicking in the snow, sniffing the tracks and racing around. From here the tracks trailed along the edge of the pines, branching off to the south.

A blustery wind blew across the frozen lake to whisper in the pines along the side of the mountain. The snow-filled boughs swayed in the gusts as Chance hurried. There was only one other cabin about a half mile down a narrow private road. His.

He began to run.

DIXIE STEPPED OUT the front door of the cabin and paused to look off to the right as she remembered the light she'd thought she'd seen the night before.

Odd. Chance had said his was the only cabin down this road and yet there was something down there in the trees that certainly looked like a cabin.

She moved to the edge of the deck and peered over the railing through the pines. A boathouse.

Her heart began to beat a little faster. That's where she'd seen the light last night. But as she stared at the boathouse, she could see that the outside light wasn't on.

Because it hadn't really been a light. It had been smaller and had gone out, more like a flashlight beam. Her mouth went dry at the thought. Someone had been down there.

The hair rose on the back of her neck. She swung around, shocked to find no one behind her. She looked into the darkness under the snow-filled pines, positive that she'd felt someone there.

"You're just jumping at shadows," she whispered to herself, wishing Chance would return. It was too quiet. And yet she sensed she was no longer alone.

Her breath came out in white puffs as she turned to look back down the mountainside through the pines to the boathouse. She was trying to tell herself that she'd just imagined the light at the boathouse last night when she saw something in the snow.

Her blood ran cold as she saw the single trail of footprints that led up from the boathouse and around the cabin. Chance's? No, she thought, her mouth going dry, because there was no sign of the dog's prints with them.

Behind her, she heard the wood creak as if someone had stepped up onto the decking.

This time when she turned, she knew the person who'd made those tracks would be standing right behind her.

Chapter Sixteen

Chance ran through the deep snow, breathing hard, his mind racing. Beauregard, thinking they were playing, had run ahead into the dense pines. He heard the dog let out a startled bark, then a yelp.

Furious with himself for not thinking to bring his gun, Chance shoved through the pine boughs, snow showering over him, and was struck hard. The blow glanced off the back of his head.

He could see his dog crouched down, hair standing up on his neck, a low growl emitting from his throat. Beauregard was staring at something behind Chance.

Bracing himself for whatever had been hiding in the trees, Chance swung around, ready to defend himself, but nothing could have prepared him for what he saw.

DIXIE COULDN'T MOVE. She couldn't turn around. The deck creaked behind her again, this time the sound so close she thought she saw a puff of frosty breath breeze past her on the wind. Fear paralyzed her because she knew what was behind her and she had no weapon. No hope.

"Dixie?"

She spun around at the sound of the voice, frowning in surprise, then smiling as she recognized the face. Her knees went weak with relief.

"Mason." She put her hand to her heart. It was beating a million beats a second. Of course her father would send Mason to get her. Mason, who always solved all her father's problems for him. "You scared me half to death. How did you find me?"

He smiled and shook his head. "I knew Beau had hired Chance Walker, so that made it somewhat easier." He glanced toward the cabin. "Tell me it's warm in that cabin. I hiked in last night, got turned around and ended up staying in someone's boathouse."

She realized that he was shivering even though he was wearing snow boots and a heavy, hooded coat and gloves. "Not exactly Texas weather, huh." She led him into the cabin, taking off her coat to toss more wood on the fire.

"Chance should be back soon," she said. "He's just gone up the road."

Mason stood by the door, looking cold, his hands buried in his coat. He was glancing around the cabin, silent, as if trying to figure out what to say to her.

"So my father sent you to take me back to Texas," she said.

"Actually…" Mason's gaze settled on her. "He doesn't know I'm here. I told him I had to go away for a few days on a business trip." He hadn't moved from near the door. He still had his hands deep in his coat pockets and he appeared to be watching for Chance.

She felt her first stirring of doubt. "Then why—"

"I thought if I came up here that we could discuss this little problem," he said, "and come to a satisfactory conciliation."

Her fear notched up a level as she looked into his eyes. She'd known Mason Roberts her whole life. He'd been at every birthday party, every family event.

He stood with the hood of his coat up, his face in shadow. It was the way he was standing. Her heart leaped to her throat as she remembered the photograph of her mother and the man. The man had put his head down, avoiding the camera, his weight on one leg, shoulders angled away. He hadn't liked having his photo taken.

Just like Mason. She thought of what few photographs she'd taken as a kid at Bonner barbecues. Mason had always managed to be in shadow or partially hidden from view by the person next to him. Mason, a man who liked to work behind the scenes, not wanting to take credit, the problem-solver and Beauregard Bonner's closest friend and associate.

Mason was studying her, a half smile on his face, eyes wary. "Come on, Dixie. You and I have always been straight with each other. Let's not play games now. You know why I'm here, don't you?"

She stared at her mother's former lover. Rebecca's father. "You bastard."

"*REBECCA?*" Chance gaped at the woman standing in the pines, a piece of tree limb in her gloved hands. He shook his head, thinking the blow to his head must have messed up his brain. "Rebecca?"

"Chance," she said in that breathless Southern accent of hers. "I didn't know it was you. I heard someone coming... Then I saw that big ol' dog."

All he could do was stare. It had been years and yet she seemed just the same. She was dressed in a suede coat with white fur, the same fur that was on her knee-high leather boots and her hat. She carried a large suede shoulder bag in the same color. Her blond hair curved around her perfectly made-up face as if she were going to breakfast at some fancy ski resort.

"What are you doing here?" he asked, wanting to laugh. She was so Rebecca. So wrong for him. So not like her sister Dixie, who was so right for him.

"Daddy told me about Dixie," Rebecca said. "I was headed for New York to do some last-minute Christmas shopping and I decided to fly to Montana instead to try to get her home for Christmas."

He didn't know what to say. This was definitely the Rebecca Bonner he remembered. Jet-setter. Fashion plate. Privileged beyond belief.

"I tried to call," she said, and glanced at the dog who was still growling. "He isn't going to bite me, is he?"

"Put down the stick," Chance told her. Beauregard quit growling. "You just scared him."

"Not as much as the two of you scared me. I'm so sorry I hit you. But when I heard something coming, I thought it might be a bear." She smiled at him just like she used to so many years ago. The years had been good to her. He figured her money and the latest antiaging techniques and supplies hadn't hurt, either.

"Bears *hibernate* in the winter," he said, and rubbed

the lump on his head, feeling a little dazed. "Why didn't you just follow the road?"

"I saw tracks coming down this way," she said. "So I followed them."

The second tracks. He glanced past her and saw that the footprints continued on down the shoreline—straight to his boathouse.

"Come on, we need to get up to the cabin," he said. "It's right up here."

Rebecca nodded and shielded her eyes to look up the hillside to the cabin. "I can't wait to see my sister."

"YOU *BASTARD!*" Blinded by her anger at what he'd done to her mother and Rebecca, Dixie grabbed up the poker from the fireplace and came at Mason, hitting him across one arm and shoulder before he could get the gun from his pocket.

He swore as he wrenched the poker from her hands and shoved the barrel end of the gun in her face. "Try me," he snapped, his hand shaking with anger. "You think I won't pull the trigger? You're *dead* wrong."

"Oh, I know too well what you're capable of," Dixie snapped. "You hired two men to kill me and I know you killed my mother to keep her from exposing you." She wanted to fly at him again but knew he *would* shoot her.

"You're mistaken, Dixie. I didn't hire anyone to kill you. I prefer to take care of problems myself. I thought you knew that about me."

She saw pain in his eyes and desperation. He didn't want to kill her. She felt confused. Why had he come here if not to keep her from exposing him? Could she be wrong about him being a killer? Then how did she explain the gun he held on her?

"You were like family," she snapped.

He laughed. "Dixie, I *am* family. Haven't you figured it out yet? My father was Earle Bonner. Just because the son of a bitch denied me the same way he did Carl…"

She heard the bitterness in his voice. The jealousy she'd seen between him and Carl. It all made sense now. "That's why you pretended to be Beauregard Bonner in Idaho."

"Don't read more into this than is there. I just used his name," Mason said. "I love your father like the brother he is."

She smirked at that. "Is that why you killed the woman he loved, my mother?"

"Your mother died in a car accident. I would imagine she couldn't face your father with the truth and found driving into the lake easier."

"That's a lie. She wouldn't have killed herself, not with two babies at home and a husband she loved," Dixie snapped. "Were you jealous because she fell in love with my father? Or was it only ever about money?"

"I made your father what he is today," Mason said. "I was the one who talked him into doing the test well on the farm. He wouldn't be anything without me."

"And you got rich right along with him."

He shook his head. "It's not the same. Beau's never understood that taking handouts from him isn't the same as being the man behind the fortune. It makes a man bitter."

"Especially if he's a thankless bastard," she said.

"Dixie, Dixie, why couldn't you have just left things alone?" Mason said in his conciliatory tone.

She heard a sound outside the cabin.

Unfortunately, Mason heard it, as well. He stepped to her, grabbing her arm as he shoved the gun into her side, shielding himself behind her as she heard the dog bark at the cabin door.

Chance. Her heart dropped. She opened her mouth to call to him, to warn him he was about to walk into an ambush. Mason clamped his hand over her mouth, the gun barrel now at her temple as he whispered, "Make a sound and the last thing your boyfriend will see is your brains blown all over his cabin."

CHANCE SAW Beauregard sniffing at two sets of tracks on the deck. He motioned for Rebecca to hang back as he flung open the cabin door. Beauregard bounded in. Chance ducked and rolled, coming up behind the couch.

In that split second, as the door swung in, he'd taken in the scene in front of the fire. His heart had dropped like a stone as he saw Dixie, the gun to her head, and Mason Roberts with his hand over her mouth. Her blue eyes were wide with fear and fury.

He came up from behind the couch just as Mason started to swing the barrel of the gun toward the dog. Dixie saw it, too, and made her move, just as Chance had known she would. She wasn't going to let Mason shoot the dog—or him. Chance could never have loved her more than at that moment.

As he leaped over the couch, Dixie elbowed Mason

in the ribs and grabbed the wrist holding the gun. The shot went wild. The gun fell to the floor, skittering away as Chance tackled Mason and took him down, Dixie falling with them onto the floor in front of the fireplace.

It all happened in an instant. Chance got a choke hold on Mason, who seemed to instantly drain of fight. Chance had an age advantage, as well as self-defense training. But still it surprised him that Mason didn't seem to have the fight of a killer.

Dixie scrambled to her feet to find the gun Mason had dropped. Chance had the man down, but she wasn't taking any chances.

At the sound of a low growl, Dixie turned to look back at Chance. He'd completely neutralized Mason, who sat against the wall breathing hard, head down, looking beaten.

Chance reached to jerk Mason to his feet, turning as Dixie did to see what Beauregard was growling about.

Dixie blinked in astonishment. "Rebecca?"

She stood just inside the front door of the cabin. In her hand was Mason's gun, the one Dixie had been looking for.

"I thought I told you to call off your dog?" Rebecca said as she leveled the gun at him.

"Beauregard," Chance ordered. "Down."

The dog stopped growling, but like everyone else in the room kept his gaze on Rebecca.

"What are you doing here?" Dixie asked.

"Didn't Chance tell you? I came to see you, little sister."

Dixie knew that sarcastic tone too well. "How long have you known?"

Rebecca smiled. "I overheard Mother and Mason arguing. What was I?" she asked Mason. "Five? I heard you threaten to kill her if she told my daddy. I heard everything you said, including how you would take me far away so she would never see me again."

Mason was looking at her, a strange expression on his face.

"You said you would kill me, you didn't care about the little snotty-nosed brat, isn't that what you said?" Rebecca continued, the gun held steady in her hand, her voice calm, no emotion in her face.

"Rebecca, put the gun away and we can talk about this," Chance said quietly. "You don't want to do anything you'll regret."

She laughed. "Believe me, I'm not going to regret it. When I heard you were in Montana, I knew what you were doing," she said to Dixie. "All those years of keeping the secret just to have you planning to tell the whole world about me and my mother and my…" Her gaze shifted to Mason. "My *father*. You would love to destroy me, wouldn't you?"

"Rebecca, that's not true. I wouldn't—"

"Shut up!" She swung the gun so it was pointed at Dixie's face. "Daddy's little girl. You think I didn't know he loved you best? He knew I was some bastard's daughter. But you—" Her voice broke. "It doesn't matter. I always knew who I really was. What I really was. My own father hated me."

Mason made a sound of denial, but it was cut off by the boom of a shot from the pistol in Rebecca's hands. Wood splintered just over Mason's head.

Dixie felt Chance step up behind her, his hands on her waist. She knew what he planned to do, felt it in his touch.

"Rebecca," Chance said. "Give me the gun. You're not a killer."

She laughed. "Wrong, Chance. Who do you think hired the men to stop my sister? I'm my daddy's daughter." Her gaze moved to Mason. "My *real* daddy's daughter."

As Chance shoved Dixie aside and launched himself at Rebecca, she swung the barrel of the gun. Dixie heard the thunder of the shot as she fell, heard the sound Mason made as the bullet found its mark.

Rebecca got off only one more shot before Chance reached her.

Dixie heard his cry of pain and scrambled to her feet in time to see her half sister hit the floor, the gun still in her hand.

Chance swung around, a look of horror on his face as he dragged Dixie into his arms, shielding her from the sight of her sister dead on the floor from a self-inflicted gunshot wound to the head.

Epilogue

That spring was the longest of Chance's life. It had snowed every day for months after Dixie had taken the jet back to Texas to be with her father.

Chance had wanted to go, but Dixie said she needed some time alone and that her father needed her. For a while, Chance called her every day, then once a week, then once a month. He knew Dixie and Beau needed to heal and that they both blamed themselves.

Beau had managed to keep the real story out of the press. As far as the public knew, the holidays had been a tragic time for the Bonner family. A burglar had broken into the Lancaster home and killed Oliver Lancaster, husband of Rebecca Bonner Lancaster, while she was away on Christmas vacation with her sister Dixie in Montana.

While there, she was tragically killed along with Beauregard Bonner's closest friend and associate, Mason Roberts.

Only Chance knew that Beau had found an envelope with his name on it on his desk weeks later when he returned to his office. It was from Mason. A confession letter filled with painful apology and regret. In the letter, Mason told Beau he was taking the jet to Montana to try to protect Dixie from Rebecca. Mason feared that Rebecca was behind Dixie's abduction, faked kidnapping, and ultimately planned to have her killed.

Carl paid off Oliver's gambling debts, keeping that part quiet from the press, and spent more time with Beau at the house. They talked a lot about Sarah.

Dixie had quit her job and taken Rebecca's and Oliver's three children and moved into her father's huge empty house. Beau had retired, selling Bonner Unlimited, and setting up trust funds for the kids. He'd realized, according to Dixie, that he had no need to make more money.

Instead he wanted to spend more time with his family. Dixie sent pictures of the kids with grandpa.

More times than he could count, Chance started a letter to Dixie, asking her to bring the children and come be his wife. But he always ended up tossing the half-written letters in the fire.

He'd thought about going to Texas and begging her to come back with him. But he couldn't ask her to leave Texas, her family and the only home the kids had known, as much as she wanted to.

One bright warm day in June, Chance took his fishing pole down to the lake, Beauregard bounding along beside him as they climbed into the boat and motored out to a favorite spot. He'd caught a few nice trout when he heard a commotion on the beach and looked back toward his cabin.

Over the winter, he'd remodeled it, adding a second floor to give himself something to do, as well as to put the memory of what had happened there far from his mind.

Now he stared toward the beach, his heart in his throat. When he'd built onto the cabin, he'd done it with the dream that maybe he could get Dixie and the kids to come up next Christmas. They could have a real Christmas with a larger tree. He'd even buy some decorations.

He knew that's all it was, a dream. He never thought he'd see Dixie Bonner in Montana again, let alone standing on his doorstep.

But as he started the motor on the boat and turned the bow toward shore, he could have sworn that was her on the beach. There were three kids playing in the water along the edge of the lake.

Beauregard barked excitedly as Chance neared the shore. He cut the engine, staring at the woman standing near his boathouse. She had her eyes shaded against the sun, but even from a distance he could see that she was smiling. Her long legs were tanned, that not-so-scrawny behind was clad in white shorts, and he could make out a peach tank top beneath that wild mane of dark curly hair that fell past her shoulders.

She hesitated only a moment, then charged toward him, splashing into the water. Beauregard plunged in, swimming to her, making a yelping sound, excited at the sight of her.

Chance laughed, took off his shirt and dove in, swimming toward her as the boat floated lazily toward shore.

He caught her in chest-high water, pulling her into

his arms. She was laughing and crying, kissing him, then pulling back to look into his eyes as if he was the best thing she'd ever seen.

"I got your letter," she said.

"My letter?"

"The one asking me to marry you, silly." She was grinning at him, mischief in her eyes.

"But I never—"

She kissed him cutting off the rest of his words. As she pulled back, she said, "But you know I would never accept a proposal unless it was in person."

"I recall." He looked into those amazing blue eyes. "Have you always known me so well?"

She grinned. "Since I was twelve and I fell madly in love with you. It was just a matter of time before you asked me to marry you. That is why you added on to the cabin, isn't it?"

He laughed. "You know it." He glanced toward the edge of the lake where Rebecca's three children stood as if waiting. They looked anxious, almost afraid of what was going to happen next. "Do they know?"

Dixie nodded. "They're just waiting for you to make it official so they can go swimming in the lake at their new home. Oh, I should mention that my father and uncle Carl plan to buy a place across the lake. They want to be close to the kids. Including the ones you and I are going to have. Still glad you sent me that letter?"

He laughed. "Marry me, Dixie Bonner, and I promise to love you and those three kids and any others we might have until death do us part."

"Just like in the letter you meant to write me," she said with a grin.

"Just like in all the letters I did write you but just didn't mail," he said as he brushed her wet hair back from her face, wondering how he could be so blessed. "Well?"

She grinned. "All I can say is...it's about time, Chance Walker." She kissed him, then let out a whoop. On the beach the kids started clapping and cheering. Then they were all in the water, the sun beating down on them, the sky bluer than blue on one of those amazing Montana summer days.

He said a prayer for his daughter and gathered his family around him, already thinking of Christmas and the homemade tinfoil silver star he'd saved to put on top of the tree.

* * * * *

New York Times *bestselling author
Linda Lael Miller is back with a new romance
featuring the heartwarming McKettrick family
from Silhouette Special Edition.*

SIERRA'S HOMECOMING
by Linda Lael Miller

*On sale December 2006,
wherever books are sold.*

Turn the page for a sneak preview!

Soft, smoky music poured into the room.

The next thing she knew, Sierra was in Travis's arms, close against that chest she'd admired earlier, and they were slow dancing.

Why didn't she pull away?

"Relax," he said. His breath was warm in her hair.

She giggled, more nervous than amused. What was the matter with her? She was attracted to Travis, had been from the first, and he was clearly attracted to her. They were both adults. Why not enjoy a little slow dancing in a ranch-house kitchen?

Because slow dancing led to other things. She took a step back and felt the counter flush against her lower back. Travis naturally came with her, since they were holding hands and he had one arm around her waist.

Simple physics.

Then he kissed her.

Physics again—this time, not so simple.

"Yikes," she said, when their mouths parted.

He grinned. "Nobody's ever said that after I kissed them."

She felt the heat and substance of his body pressed against hers. "It's going to happen, isn't it?" she heard herself whisper.

"Yep," Travis answered.

"But not tonight," Sierra said on a sigh.

"Probably not," Travis agreed.

"When, then?"

He chuckled, gave her a slow, nibbling kiss. "Tomorrow morning," he said. "After you drop Liam off at school."

"Isn't that...a little...soon?"

"Not soon enough," Travis answered, his voice husky. "Not nearly soon enough."

nocturne™

**Explore the dark and sensual
new realm of paranormal romance.**

HAUNTED
BY LISA CHILDS

**The first book in the riveting
new 3-book miniseries, Witch Hunt.**

DEATH CALLS
BY CARIDAD PIÑEIRO

**Darkness calls to humans,
as well as vampires...**

*On sale December 2006,
wherever books are sold.*

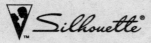

HARLEQUIN® *Romance*®

**From the Heart.
For the Heart.**

**Get swept away into the Outback
with two of Harlequin Romance's
top authors.**

Coming in December...

Claiming the Cattleman's Heart
BY BARBARA HANNAY

And in January don't miss...

Outback Man Seeks Wife
BY MARGARET WAY

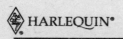

HARLEQUIN®

American ROMANCE®

IS PROUD TO PRESENT

COWBOY VET
by Pamela Britton

Jessie Monroe is the last person on earth
Rand Sheppard wants to rely on, but he needs
a veterinary technician—yesterday—and she's the
only one for hire. It turns out the woman who
destroyed his cousin's life isn't who Rand thought
she was. And now she's all he can think about!

"Pamela Britton writes the kind of
wonderfully romantic, sexy, witty romance
that readers dream of discovering
when they go into a bookstore."

—*New York Times* bestselling author
Jayne Ann Krentz

Cowboy Vet *is available from*
Harlequin American Romance in December 2006.

REQUEST YOUR FREE BOOKS!

2 FREE NOVELS
PLUS 2
FREE GIFTS!

HARLEQUIN®

INTRIGUE®

Breathtaking Romantic Suspense

YES! Please send me 2 FREE Harlequin Intrigue® novels and my 2 FREE gifts. After receiving them, if I don't wish to receive any more books, I can return the shipping statement marked "cancel." If I don't cancel, I will receive 6 brand-new novels every month and be billed just $4.24 per book in the U.S., or $4.99 per book in Canada, plus 25¢ shipping and handling per book and applicable taxes, if any*. That's a savings of close to 15% off the cover price! I understand that accepting the 2 free books and gifts places me under no obligation to buy anything. I can always return a shipment and cancel at any time. Even if I never buy another book from Harlequin, the two free books and gifts are mine to keep forever.

182 HDN EEZ7   382 HDN EEZK

Name	(PLEASE PRINT)

Address	Apt.

City	State/Prov.	Zip/Postal Code

Signature (if under 18, a parent or guardian must sign)

Mail to Harlequin Reader Service®:

IN U.S.A.
P.O. Box 1867
Buffalo, NY
14240-1867

IN CANADA
P.O. Box 609
Fort Erie, Ontario
L2A 5X3

Not valid to current Harlequin Intrigue subscribers.

Want to try two free books from another line?
Call 1-800-873-8635 or visit www.morefreebooks.com.

* Terms and prices subject to change without notice. NY residents add applicable sales tax. Canadian residents will be charged applicable provincial taxes and GST. This offer is limited to one order per household. All orders subject to approval. Credit or debit balances in a customer's account(s) may be offset by any other outstanding balance owed by or to the customer. Please allow 4 to 6 weeks for delivery.

HI06

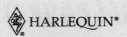 **HARLEQUIN®**

INTRIGUE

COMING NEXT MONTH

#957 FORCE OF THE FALCON by Rita Herron
Eclipse
After a string of bizarre animal attacks near Falcon Ridge,
Brack Falcon finds a woman left for dead. But protecting
Sonya Silverstein means opening his long-dormant heart.

#958 TRIGGERED RESPONSE by Patricia Rosemoor
Security Breach
Brayden Sloane is a wanted man. He remembers an accident, an
explosion. Was he responsible? Only Claire Fanshaw knows for sure,
but how will she react to his touch?

#959 RELUCTANT WITNESS by Kathleen Long
Fate brings Kerri Nelson and Wade Sorenson back together to save
the life of her son, the only witness to a heinous crime.

#960 PULL OF THE MOON by Sylvie Kurtz
He's a Mystery
She's at Moongate Mansion for a story. He thinks she's an impostor.
But before history repeats Valerie Zea and Nicholas Galloway will
have to put their doubts aside to solve the mystery behind an
heiress's kidnapping.

#961 LAKOTA BABY by Elle James
Returning soldier Joe Lonewolf must enter the ugly underbelly of his
tribe if he's to rescue the baby boy he's never seen.

#962 UNDERCOVER SHEIK by Dana Marton
When Dr. Sadie Kauffman is kidnapped by desert bandits in Beharrain,
her only salvation lies in Sheik Nasir, the king's brother, who's trying
to stop a tyrant from plunging the country into civil war.

www.eHarlequin.com

HICNM1106